ANDROMEDA SPACEWAYS

Magazine

SCIENCE FICTION, FANTASY AND HORROR

Best Stories: Vol. 5

PUBLISHED BY

ANDROMEDA SPACEWAYS PUBLISHING INCORPORATED

WWW.ANDROMEDASPACEWAYS.COM

MARCH 2023

Subscriptions
Buy a First Class Ticket at *andromedaspaceways.com/subscribe* and get brand-new fiction in EPUB, MOBI or PDF formats.

Submissions
ASM is open to science fiction, fantasy and supernatural horror works up to 10,000 words in length. Please read the submission guidelines and access the Submissions Manager at *andromedaspaceways.com/submissions-manager*.

CONTENTS

INTRODUCTION

Nick Marone

Have you ever plotted a course and scheduled your space jumps with the utmost care, only to find that a black hole has sent you lightyears away from your intended destination? Well, that's sort of what happened with the *Best Stories: Vol. 5* anthology. Maybe the star charts were off. Or maybe the Sourge-That-Shall-Not-Be-Named disrupted our plans. Despite our rather circuitous route around the galaxy, our ship has now finally returned to its original course. Now, in 2022, ASM has the honour of presenting to you the *Andromeda Spaceways Magazine Best Stories: Vol. 5* anthology!

This anthology collects thirteen of the best stories from ASM's 2020 issues (#78–81). It was tough choosing from among the forty-four published in that year, but I think we have made some great choices. In fact, one of the featured stories, Nikky Lee's "Dingo and Sister", took out two Aurealis Awards for 2020—the Best Fantasy Novella and Best Adult Short Story categories.

ASM is a small team of dedicated speculative fiction fans, and I'd like to extend my thanks to all who were involved in getting these stories to publication. A special thanks goes to the editors of Issues #78 (Brooke Munday), #79 (Joel Schanke and Mallory Thomas), #80 (Tom Dullemond), and #81 (Laura Cesile and Tom Dullemond again) for their hard work curating the pickings of the slush readers.

Speaking of slush readers, please share with me as I give a round of applause to our team of volunteer readers for their tireless efforts. They read hundreds of stories in 2020, helping the editors find the most suitable stories for the magazine. ASM is one of only a few magazines to offer personalised feedback for submitted stories—we are proud of that and deeply appreciate our slush readers, as well as our dedicated Submissions Manager,

But of course, the highest thanks goes to the authors for creating such enjoyable stories. It is our hope that you keep on writing and that your creativity continues to reach new heights. And if you have not yet been selected for publication in ASM or another magazine, remember that a rejection only means to send us something else—keep trying!

THE ETHNOGRAPHER

Grace Chan

Featured in Issue #79

I STEP DOWN FROM THE *Linnaeus* into a crimson haze creased with shadows. The wind howls like a banshee symphony. At once, I understand why the Vullon have no hearing organs: the noise of this alien planet inspires madness.

I brace myself against the ship, praying that my Terra-Suit's rattling joints will hold. The wind changes with a roar. I stagger, but the implants in my left leg adjust to keep me from falling.

Out of the dust, three figures approach along a wide concourse. Although I've seen them dozens of times in hologram, the bodies of the Vullon surprise me with their reptilian beauty. The last aliens I studied were not so pleasant to the senses, despite my best efforts to get used to the slime and the smell. I had to keep my regulator at max empathy for the 12 months I lived with them.

As they near, I recognise Ambassador Cuvo's green painted face. The name, of course, is a synaesthetic translation, just as *Vullo* approximates the name they give their planet.

They are smaller than I'd expected. Pentagonal armour covers their torsos in perfect tessellation. Close-up, I notice that beneath the paint, their faces are also filigreed in miniature scales.

Cuvo lifts their upper limbs and signs an introduction. *Welcome, Egal, scientist/ scholar of the humans. You are the first of your kind to walk among us. We are glad/honoured to receive you.*

My neuro-plus shifts into gear, accessing the linguistic files that I honed during the seven-month journey from Mars to Vullo. I sign self-consciously, my fingers clumsy inside thick gloves. *Thank you, Cuvo. I am glad/honoured to arrive.*

Cuvo makes a gesture of deference. *You and I have many ideas/questions. But you are tired from your travels. We will go to a dark/comfortable place and you will rest and eat. Can you breathe/pray?*

I wait for my neuro-plus to translate Cuvo's swift movements.

Not yet, I sign to the alien. *My analytics tell me it will take 34 Vullon days for my body to acclimatise.*

Our scientists/scholars can help you with that.

Cuvo signals. The other two Vullon, whose faces are unpainted, take my luggage. I look back at the *Linnaeus*. She has already pleated her heat shields against her flanks and powered down for hibernation. A dust cover unfolds over her silver body. A sensation of loss stirs my chest. I turn my regulator up a notch, and the feeling dims.

We walk along the concourse without any notion of rushing. The wind batters me from above; gravity drags at my bones. Cuvo stays at my side. I feel the eyes of the other two—gigantic, close-set eyes the colour of rainclouds—poring over me.

How do you travel on Vullo? I ask. I fumble the sign for travel and have to repeat it.

*Most of the time we walk. We also have—*Cuvo signs a word that my files don't recognise. Cuvo points to the sky. A cluster of oval shaped objects hang in the air, beneath a blanket of violet clouds. I make out the blue glow of ion engines. Ion-powered blimps? I mirror Cuvo's symbol, and Cuvo gestures affirmative.

The concourse joins another, wider and perpendicular. Several Vullon bustle around, pushing floating trolleys of equipment. A Vullon with a blue painted face directs them. A creature shaped like a giant spider is repairing a pothole.

The concourse slopes down into a desert basin, where a bustle of movement and artificial light extends to the horizon, further than my cooped-up brain can comprehend.

I kneel and take a handful of dirt between my gloved fingers. From afar, I'd thought the soil rust red, but up close I can see it has a purplish hue. I'm sweating heavily inside the tight seal of my Terra-Suit. Cuvo walks ahead, not noticing that I've stopped.

I glance up. Flame-coloured clouds swirl across an indigo sky. A bloated orange sun hangs three handspans above the horizon, a ghostly twin half reflected in my helmet's glass dome. It is late in the Vullon day. I take a steadying breath and follow Cuvo into the alien city.

◆

My name is Egal Tyro. I'm Martian and human. I'm an ethnographer. My skill is the deliberate exercise of empathy. By living within and amongst, I seek true understanding: verstehen.

Many human ethnographers work in pairs or small teams. I haven't done so for many years. In a group, you create an otherness, a space they can't enter. Alone, you have no walls. You must allow yourself to be subsumed and absorbed in order to survive.

The basin of Vo is a sprawling network of nodes and tunnels—above the surface, burrowing into the ground, invading the cliffs around the rim. I'm given quarters on the west edge of the basin, near a blimp terminal and the government district. From my window high on the cliff face, the buildings of Vo are a congregation of bowed heads, huddled against the fierce gales.

Cuvo takes me around, explaining that this is Vullon's centre of commerce and power. We visit government nodes, public squares, marketplaces, schools. Everywhere I go, they come to gawk at me.

I tell Cuvo, *I can't study if everyone looks at me.*

Cuvo gestures an apology. *I will chide/speak to them.*

Cuvo takes me to the Sentencing House. From the main street, we descend a sloping passageway stationed at intervals with white painted guards. Within gloomy chambers, defendants are brought to trial before a panel of 13 judges. The process bears some resemblance to the human system, although the judges are remarkably passive, observing the proceedings without a flicker of emotion on their yellow painted faces, and passing verdicts with little conferring. The punishments are retaliatory: solitary confinement, prescribed beatings, or surgical removal of armoured plates. *There is no death penalty,* Cuvo tells me, *but occasionally a criminal has died during the worst of the beatings.*

Cuvo takes me to a sparring arena. The noise of several thousand aliens marching into the stands makes my blood thrum. No one can hear what I hear. Within their silent world, the Vullon feel the vibrations of their mineral bodies striking the ground but are oblivious to the deafening ruckus.

Two Vullon circle one another without weapons, darting in for a brief strike, a frenzied tussle, then darting out again to dance the perimeter of the arena. The contest is excruciating. Both fighters lunge and stagger, dripping blood. Just before dusk falls, the darker scaled Vullon pins the other to the ground. The one beneath writhes for long minutes before falling still, limbs raised, tender underbelly exposed in defeat. The arena vibrates with stamping fans.

I sit in on government meetings. Governors fill the circular stands of a stone chamber. Local governors have their faces painted light green. Territorial governors, and those with special roles, like Cuvo, wear dark green paint.

In my first session, several governors address me directly. They thank humans for sharing ion engine tech, which has allowed the Vullon to venture into the air and space. I thank them for sharing their low precipitation farming breakthroughs.

By now, my skill with the Vullon sign language has improved enough that I no longer notice my neuro-plus filling in the gaps. Their written language, however, which has over three thousand symbols and is based on the shapes of their sign language, is more difficult to grasp. Even with the neuro-plus, I struggle to comprehend the lengthy policy documents.

During one meeting, a small sized Vullon, face painted light green, ascends the central podium.

I am Joul, the creature signs. *As you know, I represent the—*

Here the creature makes a sign I do not recognise. I scan through my brain. The sign translates roughly as *Mimon,* but this means nothing to me.

I turn to Cuvo, but the Ambassador is frowning down at a document.

I turn back to the speaker. Joul's eyes are unusually dark. The pentagonal plates on Joul's body also look wrong. Instead of standing flat and sharp, they droop over the limbs.

Suddenly, I realise that the creature does not have armour at all. Beneath a special garment made to resemble a Vullon's exoskeleton, Joul is an entirely different species.

I look around the chamber. How had I not noticed it before? A few other governors are like Joul: smaller, lacking scales, draped in garments to render their difference less obvious.

I find Cuvo's gaze and signal a question. Cuvo glances away.

◆

I've been on Vullo for eight weeks. I'm starting to dream of Vullon faces instead of human faces. Their angular bodies, their rainstorm eyes, the slight gestures that convey irritation, congeniality, irony, are more proximal to me now than human behaviour. Lately, I startle on seeing my own reflection—watery eyes embedded in tender, raw skin, abutted by curling ears. Bizarre. Alien.

On a Day of Gratitude, Cuvo takes me to a sacred place deep within the rim cliffs. We are accompanied by two other governors: Nuuv, a lively individual with mottled scales, who oversees interterritorial relations; and Olon, a reserved, older Vullon who has served as a treasurer for decades.

As we walk into the windowless chamber, fragrant smoke billows into our faces. The smoke clears to reveal a stone altar, tended by a single initiate with a red painted face. The initiate glances at me sidelong. They hadn't been eager to let me enter their temple.

Our clicking footsteps float up into the shadowy void. The far wall is carved with vertical, wavy lines extending more than ten times my height. As we approach, I see that the lines are air vents.

The three governors inhale the earthy air, their bodies shivering in reverence. I stand behind and watch. Are they praying? Their shapes seem sharply outlined, like holograms with the contrast dialled up to maximum.

A film descends over Cuvo's grey eyes. My skin prickles.

What/who do you worship? I ask later, as we're walking around the chamber.

Cuvo gestures slowly. *The Unseen God, who dwells in/births the middle of the world and breathes life-giving winds.*

You bathe in the God-breath?

An affirmative sign, but stiffly—perhaps I've trespassed, by putting language to the preverbal. *The breath of the Unseen God gives us wisdom/spirit.*

The term is difficult, implying the essence of the soul rather than simple knowledge. I wonder if I can be given the Unseen's breath. I suspect not.

There's a commotion at the entrance. The initiate is speaking to a smaller figure. The newcomer has the reddish skin and dark eyes of a Mimon. Both the initiate and the newcomer wave their limbs wildly. Then the newcomer walks away.

What happened? I ask.

Cuvo turns and stops, and the other two governors stop too. *It is not custom/good/proper for Mimon to worship here.*

They aren't allowed in?

This is a sacred place. The Mimon have their own gods. We do not go into their temples.

Where are their temples?

Not in Vo, says Nuuv. *The Mimon are many, but they don't spend much time here.*

Are they not Vullon?

Not Vullon like us, says Cuvo. *Equal, but different.*

We once confused equality with sameness/uniformity, adds Olon. *Now we realise that some differences should not be concealed/overcome, but celebrated.*

Differences?

We are not alike. The Mimon are fiercer/fickler. It is not in their nature to toil as we do. We grow our food in labs, they hunt and forage. We train scientists/

scholars and traders, they train crafters and builders. *Just as we do not want to work the land, they do not want to sit in chambers. Joul and their kind need to stop fighting about nothing.*

I picture Joul and the other Mimon sitting in the government hall, draped in camouflage. Unexpectedly, I'm filled with sadness.

What are they fighting for?

Nuuv gestures impatience. *They have the right to work and employ, to trade, to enrol in school and to serve/sit on government. We have given them as much as we can. We're not sure what else they want.*

I hesitate. *Do you regard them as equal in wisdom/spirit?*

The Mimon are equal in every way, says Cuvo.

Nuuv and Olon gesture agreement.

Do not mistake us, Egal Tyro. We uphold/respect them. Joul, and many before Joul, endured entrenched discrimination from our predecessors. But it is time for them to recognise that things are different now.

There is something in Cuvo's movements that I can't interpret. Even though I can hear, I feel like a child watching adults talk over my head.

I understand, I say.

We leave the temple, descend through a maze of tunnels and emerge onto the basin flats. A squall screeches down from the dusk sky, swelling my ears, and I crave the quiet of the temple: just the hiss of smoke and the gentle tapping of mineral scales on stone.

Nuuv and Olon signal a polite farewell and depart. Cuvo walks with me through the streets to my quarters. My bionic leg aches. Cuvo slows to match my pace.

You have been a perfect host, I say. *You impress me with your steadfastness/patience.*

Cuvo shifts into a questioning stance.

I'd like to spend some time with the Mimon.

Cuvo looks up at the moons. Tonight, three are visible: two close together, blush tinted, and a solitary white-blue orb, just above the cliff heads.

I knew you would ask this, Egal Tyro. It is not a custom/good/proper idea, but I will not stop you.

◆

I emerge from the blimp terminal into a dark, lush land. Indigo plants with leaves as large as my body rustle between irregular rock formations. The soil smells old and loamy. Here, the winds do not roar, but mutter and moan.

Panting, I lurch through the strange forest, my automated left leg a fraction faster than my right, no matter how hard I try to balance my gait. I'm out of my Terra-Suit; I have been for several weeks now. My red blood cells have enlarged to absorb more oxygen from the nitrogen heavy air, and my muscle fibres have grown to tolerate the higher gravity. Injections have thickened my skin to protect me from the scalding winds. My body has become less human and more Vullon.

A winding path takes me to a clearing where the rocky pinnacles have been hollowed into buildings. A group of Mimon are packing boxes into an underground refrigeration system. Another group are weaving string from stuff that looks like dried reeds, while another flit around a low stone table, preparing a feast. Their skin is the colour of dunes at dusk, their eyes ink black and spaced far apart.

Tentatively, I move into the settlement, gesturing a greeting. No one responds. A rush of irritation and panic heats my palms. My regulator dials up, and the fear dampens.

At last, a Mimon with deeper, purplish skin approaches me.

Crave/yearn?

My mouth waters at the smells wafting towards me. I follow the Mimon to the stone table, which is laden with strange food: a starchy cake baked from the flesh of a seedpod, a stew that tastes like cashews, and a cool milky drink made from seedpod juice. I eat my fill, listening to the wind ululating across the pinnacle tops, observing the Mimon as they observe me. They touch hands often but hardly talk. I wonder at their silence.

After the sun sets, the first Mimon takes me into a building and shows me to a room where a bed has been assembled for me.

What is your name? I ask.

The Mimon hesitates.

I am Egal Tyro.

I know.

The Mimon leans forward and seizes my arm. A light, brisk tapping touches the inside of my wrist. I freeze.

My name, says the alien, releasing me.

Stunned, I realise that they weren't silent over dinner after all. The Mimon language is tactile. A shiver spreads from my wrist, up my arm, and across my entire body. The pattern—the name—impresses itself, like a flower unfurling, on the walls of my mind.

◆

After I've been with the Mimon for a week, Joul comes to speak with me.

So, you are the alien.

I'm sitting on a flat rock, peeling strips of fibrous husk from seedpod shells. I place the shell in my lap and make a symbol for greeting with recognition.

Why have you come to us? Joul asks.

My wish is to understand the Vullon.

We are not Vullon.

Is that what you say, or what they say?

A film closes over Joul's black eyes. Without face paint and camouflaging garments, the Mimon looks smaller, sharper, more agile.

What did the Ambassador tell you, alien?

Cuvo said you are not Vullon like them.

A laugh shakes Joul's body. Of course. *They have stolen/claimed the name of our world. If we are not Vullon, how can we be equal as they say we are?*

Why are you so angry?

Another laugh, less pleasant. *Walk with me.*

I climb to my feet, fibrous tendrils falling from my lap. My leg is stiff from sitting. Joul strides ahead, quick and nimble, picking a path across the rocky plateau. It's near the height of day. The sun shows its swollen amber face between banks of muddy clouds.

I have lived in Vo for a long time, signs Joul, when I catch up. *It always feels eerie/nostalgic to come home. Like an old dream that I'm not sure is mine, or one that someone told me about when I was young.*

Joul's words transport me abruptly to the red landscape of Mars. An ache blooms in my chest, but my regulator scoops it up.

I have two jobs, Joul continues. *Does that surprise you? I am a governor, as you know. But after I finish my meetings, I mind Vullon children. Some would say I am being greedy. I am lucky to have a respected/proper job and to move in elite circles. But if I want to give money to my family, it is not enough.*

Then I look around. Why are the other child-minders also Mimon? Why are the cleaners, servers, labourers and sex workers also Mimon? Is it because of our temperament, as the Vullon like to say?

Lines of anger sear up and down Joul's body, sparking off my mirror-neurons, scorching the underside of my skin.

Joul turns to me. *You are an unusual one. You enjoy being an alien, observing others. You blur the edges of your self. You wish to be ingested into an alien society. Ingested/digested/dissolved.*

My cheeks flush, and my regulator intensifies.

Temperament is an indefensible word, isn't it? I offer.

Joul laughs again, limbs trembling with bitterness. We slow as the land begins to pitch downhill.

Where are we going?

I will show you something, alien scientist/scholar.

We walk for another half an hour without speaking. Above a distant line of mountains, clouds gather into a dark mass. A lightning storm is brewing. At last, we come to a dusty valley, where a large stone building overlooks a plantation of seedpods. Small figures move up and down the trellised rows, tending to the crops. Two Mimon rest in the shade of the building, sitting flank to flank, limbs entwined. Talking.

This is a healing centre, Joul signs to me. *Mimon who have been harmed by Vullon come here to recover.*

I peer at the resting Mimon. One of them is disfigured, with a scarred face. My gut twists. *How many live here?*

About one hundred, but there are many such centres.

Are the Vullon aware of this?

Of course. But they say it is only a minority who have these violent tendencies. And they say they have their own centres, with their own victims.

A sour taste floods my mouth. *Is that true?*

You ask the wrong questions, silly alien. The right question is: who holds power/ reality? Why is it that my friend down there, whose face was scarred by acid, can do nothing but accept this fate?

To my surprise, a child detaches itself from the hip of one of the Mimon, runs into the crop and wriggles beneath the trellis. The indigo plants shiver.

Can a child be mixed-race?

Careful, Egal—you will offend someone's delicate sensibilities. Yes, a child can be mixed, but they will be regarded as one of us.

Joul takes my arm gently. One limb taps the inside of my wrist, pressing words into my skin. Another continues to draw words in the air. *If you want to know us, alien, you must bridge/leap this gap.*

Language.

Language. Feeling.

Feeling?

Take down those blocks in your brain. The ones that dam up your feelings.

Dry lightning crackles over our heads. Down in the plantation, the child races into the open valley, kicking up a cloud of dark dust. As the cloud rises into the air, a strange lightness lifts my chest. Joul is right.

I lower my regulator. Waves of pain ram into me. I see the Mimon, sequestered in their remote towns, conveniently unseen and unheard. I see the scarred ones, silenced and shut away, and the children who will one day understand that they should not have been born. I see Joul, black eyes burning with rage, dust shrouded body twitching with helplessness and sorrow.

"I'm sorry," I whisper aloud, and although Joul can't hear me, there is an understanding. Joul holds on to my wrist as a torrent of tears sweeps me away.

◆

You shouldn't go with Joul.

Groggily, I open my eyes. The sky is dark, with a hint of dawn in the east. The purple skinned Mimon from my first day here, months ago now, is leaning over me.

You shouldn't go with Joul, the Mimon repeats. The words crackle up my arm.

Why not?

Joul is…brave/strong. But this is too much. There is no need to stir up such controversy.

I sit up, pushing my blankets aside. *No need?*

The Vullon will see us as troublemakers. A lot of us think it would be better not to offend.

You are happy with the way things are, then?

The Mimon squeezes my arm. *A generation ago, things were difficult. But I count myself fortunate. I have enough.*

I tap out my words, hardly needing my neuro-plus. *Let go of me.*

The Mimon releases me and retreats, shivering with rejection.

In the morning, I board a blimp with Joul and five other Mimon. We rise into a strong northerly. The blimp shudders and creaks, ion engines blazing. I cling to my harness, suppressing waves of nausea.

Joul comes to me across the bay, moving easily from one handhold to the next. *Float/move with the wind, alien.*

We clasp arms and laugh.

Are you sure you want to stand/journey with us, Egal Tyro?

Yes.

It won't be easy.

I already said yes.

Joul shifts into a grateful stance. *Did you have any struggles like this, where you come from?*

I think about Earth and Mars. *Things are simpler for humans. Although our planets have many species, our kind are the most intelligent/dominant. Still, the other species have protections. Within humans...centuries ago, there were inequalities. But we've worked hard to resolve them...*

I stop talking. Joul's body is suddenly angled away from me, eyes downcast. Unease gnaws at my bones.

Within a few hours, the basin of Vo drifts into view, a dark blanket unrolling beneath a pale sky. We wait for clearance before descending through an open arena and landing on a platform with a soft thump. Clamps engage the base of the blimp and the exit gangway lowers.

Before we disembark, Joul gathers the group into a circle. We link limbs, transmitting Joul's message from body to body.

They will leer and shout and call us vile names. Shake it off like dust after a windstorm. We do this so our children/kin might live without shame.

The door opens, and the Mimon walk out of the blimp. I follow close behind. The terminal is crowded with people, mostly Vullon but also some Mimon, moving along the tunnels, sitting on benches, queuing at stalls for fried dough cakes and cheap gemstones. We take the tunnel leading towards the school, where Joul is scheduled to give a public speech about the role of attire in assimilation.

Joul has decided to give the speech without camouflage robes. The five other Mimon walking with us are also unclothed. It takes a few minutes for anyone to notice, but when they do, outrage ripples through the crowd. Space clears around us as bystanders step back. A teacher steers a group of children away, shielding their view.

You lot are crass/foul.

This is tasteless.

Take your ugly bodies out of our city.

The Mimon walk on at a steady pace. We leave the terminal and emerge onto a main thoroughfare lined with colourful shops. A pair of guards trail us. I glance back. Their white painted faces bob through the crowd, closing the gap. Sweat breaks out on my skin.

We're nearing the school when a Vullon darts into the group of Mimon. A scuffle breaks out. I rush forward, but it's over in seconds. Joul lies motionless on the ground. Blood, thick and black, spills from a hole like an eye.

A break in the crowd, torn by the attacker's escape. I launch into pursuit. The Vullon weaves down the main street, green veined scales glinting in the neon shop lights.

"Stop!" I scream, over and over, but no one can possibly hear me.

The attacker plunges into a maze of alleys. Jolts of pain wrack my left leg. Even as the Vullon draws further away, the green veined scales are burnt into my vision. I'm too weak, too slow.

I skid around a corner, nearly falling over. An empty lane. I double back, hunting for the marbled armour. Nothing.

After I catch my breath, I walk back as fast as I can, limping heavily. A crowd has gathered—the pale guards, a passing governor, and a flock of fascinated onlookers. My breath roars in my lungs, in my ears, as I thread between mineral bodies, to the eye of the storm. Joul is already dead.

♦

Six months after I first arrived on Vullo, I return to my ship.

The *Linnaeus* is exactly where I left her, at the end of the concourse, covered in a thick layer of dust. I touch her smooth flank. When I lift my hand, the dust peels away, revealing part of a red circle surrounded by white stars: the logo of the Martian Interstellar Exploration Program.

A gust sweeps down, flinging sheets of dust from the ship. I cower under her belly and squeeze my eyes shut against the sting. The wind is symphonic: a thousand voices, unheard by anyone but by the human, pitched high and low, whispering secrets into my bruised ears. I strain to make out their meaning, but the words dissolve into nonsense.

A familiar ache shudders through my leg. I'll have to service the implants when I get back to Mars; I've neglected them for too many months. My knee can no longer extend to its full range, and when I try to run, pain jolts into my hip.

I could wake the *Linnaeus* with a single command. She would fold away her dust cover, open her hatch and extend a ladder for me to climb into her cool interior. Within an hour, I could be rising into the atmosphere, never to lay eyes on a Vullon or a Mimon again.

I crawl out from beneath the *Linnaeus*, favouring my sore leg. I look down at the rough, scaly skin of my adapted hands. I press the wrinkled pads of my fingers together. They no longer look like my hands, or even human hands.

I look back towards Vo. Long bands of clouds, backlit by the rising sun, touch the far rim. As the sun climbs into the sky, the basin shifts through a series of colours: violet-black to ochre-brown to blood-red. The blue face of the last moon sinks behind the cliffs. I breathe deeply, inhaling the smells of sand and fire.

"Not quite yet, my dear," I tell my ship.

Limping slowly, I walk back to Vo. I descend the wide concourse that terrified me the first day I set foot on Vullo. Now largely ignored, I weave through the throng of mineral bodies, following the main street to the Sentencing House.

A group of Mimon are hovering outside. I recognise some of them, and we exchange symbols of greeting. The white faced guards step aside to let me in. I walk down the tunnel and follow the press of bodies into the trial chamber.

The circular pews are already crowded with Vullon and Mimon. The trial of

Joul's murderer has stirred up a great deal of public outcry. Ambassador Cuvo and the old treasurer are in the front row, speaking covertly, their limbs close together. At first, they don't notice me. Then, as I'm halfway down the aisle, Cuvo glances up. Our eyes meet across the space. After a pause, the Ambassador gestures recognition with deference—an echo of our first meeting. Unexpectedly moved, I return the gesture.

I consider going to Cuvo, but the front rows are already crowded with governors. I navigate the circumference of the chamber until I find a space at the end of a pew. I squeeze myself in next to a large Vullon, who looks at me and says nothing.

A door below the podium opens. I check my enhancements. My regulator has been off for days now. A guard steps through, and then the murderer, armour bright with veins of green. My lungs chafe and my leg aches, in abrupt memory of that frantic chase.

They climb the stone steps to the podium, the guard following a few languid paces behind. A single guard and no chains. A knot of anger congeals in my throat.

The door opens again. Thirteen judges, sombre and yellow faced, file through in a single line. Bile fills my mouth as I see that all 13 are Vullon. I hadn't expected any different, had I? But my eyes have been adapted, transformed. I am part human, part Vullon and part Mimon, and my whole being burns with rage.

AND HER LIPS TURNED TO STONE

Rachel Brittain

Featured in Issue #78

THE FOREST IS ALIVE—THAT'S what people say in town while they haggle over a bag of rice. Trees whisper late at night, the lost souls of all the people left behind after the meltdown. Nobody warned them, just left them behind to wither and die and grow back again, but what do you expect from government types?

There were other rumours, too. How a bear-man walked out of the trees one spring, shaking ice from his fur, and howled late into the night as his hair fell out and his skin bubbled and blistered. How a witch-woman deals in the souls of little girls who wander too far from home, and nothing—not even an axe or a shotgun—can keep you safe once she's picked you from the crowd.

That was the problem, living at the edge of the woods—you never knew what was true and what was tall tales and gossip.

But when the rain came down blistering or the babies came out missing hands or legs or full up with extra organs growing outside their little bodies, everybody knew why: because the exploded power plant cleared the land from the Ozarks on down through the Ouachitas. They said it was contaminated all the way to Lake Pontchartrain, and that was certifiable truth.

Another rumour: a lost girl, skin pebbled hard as stone, turned on that woodwitch—burned right through her human heart and left her for dead. Led a line of girls back to town behind her, so they say.

But these stories are never as simple as that, are they? Really, there were two girls—both wandered into the forest that day. Town whispered for years, conjuring theories on what happened out there. How the one came back and the other never did. How they'd probably succumbed to fallout a few miles in, one a little forest-funny and the other out there growing mushrooms. Made about as much sense as the truth. More maybe.

The best place to propagate half-truths is in rumours, grow them up until they take root. The full truth was this: Marelle wasn't the first girl lost, but Kadie—Kadie would be the last.

◆

Late fall meant apple harvest, meant sorting through the Winesaps and Collins Reds and Arkansas Blacks—tossing any funny ones that set off the dosimeters to find those still good to eat. Half the town gathered up, sorting and sorting, maybe sneaking a taste or two as they went. Some apples would be eaten over the next few weeks and the rest canned and preserved for winter, which came and went without too much lingering most years.

Which is when this girl went and walked out of the woods.

She had sticks in her hair and all, but Kadie still recognised her, not a day changed from the sixteen she was back when she went missing. Five years come and gone since. Kadie's own hair grew long and then was chopped off to make her work tinkering with old, pre-exclusion devices easier: mechanical things everyone said weren't worth their weight in scrap, but still came in useful when somebody needed help with broken locks or old sewing machines.

All that time since their schoolyard days, but she still recognised Marelle.

They'd been in class together long enough. Quiet little Kadie with her braids and her limp and her moon eyes watching, always watching. Hoping. Longing. Before Marelle'd up and disappeared, of course. And Kadie left behind to grow out of the braid and into her limp.

Here she was again. The last girl to go missing. The first to ever come back.

Kadie was holding a Winesap in one hand and Geiger counter in the other, the little thing beeping away, but everybody stopped their working because a girl had just walked out of the forest. And that wasn't natural.

Wasn't natural at all.

Their eyes locked, uncanny. Kadie rooted there like some old Grecian statue with hands upturned in offering. Everybody else dropped their apples. A few started over to help because even if she was unnatural it was still the neighbourly thing.

They took her in all right, but that didn't stop the talk. Whispers she'd spent too long out in the woods, had gone bad with radiation. Whispers she was back with malintent. Whispers just like the same old small-town prejudice Kadie was accustomed to, growing up on the edge of the woods.

So everyone gave her a wide berth; lost girls didn't just return unscathed like that. No burns or rotted out teeth or brain-muddled talk. Radiation did funny things. Couldn't trust it to turn everybody the same. Five long summers and winters in the forest couldn't leave a body unchanged, even if you didn't know how. That's how they told it.

Kadie watched from a distance as Marelle spun this story about an intolerable, intractable, insatiable need to get away—to get past the area of exclusion, past the stories and the millisieverts of radiation. How she made it through the woods, found another town with other people—not so different, but just different enough—on the other side. How she was going back.

"I could take you," she told Kadie one day, and the steady thump-thump-thump of her heart answered: get-away-get-away-get-away.

She pushed a strand of hair back from her face, smearing grease. "When?"

♦

Like Chernobyl and Fukushima and Lake Karachay before, there were places you didn't go if you didn't want to die. That simple. Like the forest outside of town that everyone knew soaked up more radiation than almost anywhere and cut them off from everything up north.

Every time anyone from town ventured in to find white oyster mushrooms or gather up loose firewood, they'd watch their dosimeters, tally up the RAD and scurry back if it got too close to lethal LD50.

All Kadie took was a bag with the few things worth weighing her down: an old book, cover worn off, her precious medicine, a broken compass attached to some sentimental notion of her father before the cancer got him, some rations. That was all.

The orange glow of the morning sun lit the way. Leaves crackled underfoot. How many times had she trailed the edge of the forest, foraging? And here she might never see this side of it again.

Marelle set a hurried pace and Kadie limped along behind her, slowed by this interesting piece of lichen or that gnarled root she could prop her cane against to rest for a moment. Her hips and knees ached with the walking. The town grew small behind them.

She traced a finger along the peeling bark of an old Loblolly Pine.

"People say they're alive, you know—back home."

She looked up, and Marelle had stopped. Was staring.

"People say a lot of things."

About you, Kadie thought. But all she'd wanted was to make conversation or get a reaction and she hadn't gotten one. Marelle held out a hand and Kadie took it. The forest wasn't what she had expected, so far as she had expected anything. Something oozing, maybe. Something more.

They didn't get very far. Marelle held out an arm to stop, but she didn't need the warning. The *shh-shh* of movement in the brush was enough. A fox, lean and lithe and two-headed, skidded ahead of them, both sets of lips pulled back in mirror snarls.

Kadie gasped. She'd heard tell of the animals left living since the meltdown, the ones that hadn't died right away with the patches of trees burned red. Unnatural. Mutated strange.

It lowered its back to menace, crying out in that strangled high pitch peculiar to foxes, now two voices in tandem. Doubly eerie.

"Get," Marelle told it. She picked up a rock and hurled with precision. The right head, pelted good, flinched back with a soft cry, while the left snarled something fierce. Kadie brandished her cane, waving like she intended to strike.

The fox screeched again, but when Marelle raised another rock high, the thing tucked tail and went running. She unfurled her hand—a chunk of iron-stained quartz—and considered a moment, before letting it slip back to the ground. Kadie tracked the solid, earthy thunk of it.

She stared after the fox, then pocketed the rock and hurried to follow Marelle, already moving forward. They didn't speak again until they came to the bodies.

♦

Kadie stopped—had to—rummaging in her bag for the pills. She'd misjudged the walking, how much and the pain of it. Leaning against a stunted tree, she dry-swallowed, hoping she wouldn't be left behind halfway through the forest when her legs refused to go any further.

She shifted. Her Geiger counter had been complaining all this time, an incessant mockingbird, so she'd shoved it to the bottom. It was quiet now. Maybe they'd gotten through the epicentre, past the worst of the radiation.

Illogical, of course. The deeper and darker it got, the closer to the old power plant, the worse the radiation. Did her skin tingle? DNA mutating, dying one strand after another? Or maybe just the breeze through the leaves.

She turned back to face Marelle, but found another girl. Another face, rather. Because the tree she was leaning against wasn't a tree. It was a person, covered over in moss and lichen, hard as stone. Kadie stumbled back, barely catching herself before Marelle grabbed her elbow. She was staring at the frozen girl, too.

And it wasn't just one girl—dozens of them, lining the circle of trees, and what she had thought were trees. Perfectly lifelike statues. A forest of frozen bodies.

Kadie thought of all the stories she'd heard. All the stories she'd dismissed. Thought, "Woodwitch," though she didn't mean to speak it aloud. Marelle gave her a sharp look. She was already moving past them, though, through the trees and on her way.

Real people. Real girls stolen by the witch—more than rumour—their expressions preserved in horror or grief like insects trapped in so much amber.

One girl's mouth gaped wide, another turned away, holding up a hand to fend something away. Kadie reached out as if to brush the one she'd leaned against, hands covering her face like a crying child.

The last girl to disappear before Marelle—Marcie—was lost over a decade ago. Kadie had been barely ten at the time, had just lost her father. She hadn't really paid attention. She wished she could remember the girl's face. Wished she could tell if it was her hiding behind those hands.

"Just a bit farther," said Marelle.

Kadie turned. Marelle was lovely—in a careless, forest-worn kind of way— hair a tangle of curls and face flushed ruddy. It was the one difference between the Marelle of before and the Marelle of today, this sense that she was a thing of the forest now. Kadie saw it in the tiny leaves in her hair and the mottled, mushroomy flush of her cheeks.

Their eyes caught, Kadie watching, Marelle noticing the watching. Something tugged deep in her stomach, hunger mixed with hesitation. Surrounded by dead girls—or, not quite dead, but not quite alive either—Marelle stepped forward.

It wasn't until Marelle placed a hand over Kadie's heart—firm, pressing, and she thought for a moment, just a moment, *oh, she felt it too*—that the burning, which spread through her veins like fire and flared out across her skin, took hold. Marelle's hand lingered, then fell away.

Action and reaction—it didn't connect. Marelle looked sorry, and Kadie still didn't understand why. Until she blinked down. And saw: the sloping expanse of her own body laid out underneath her, changing, shifting. A touch and a response—equal and opposite. So very, very opposite.

Verdant green spread like infection—her whole body gone septic. A delicate flush of moss. It sprouted from her pores and grew and grew. The burning spread, immolating her body from the inside out, every muscle stiffening, every cell turned hard with rigor—living dead.

Her cane clattered down, sound muffled on a bed of decaying leaves. A noise of desperate dissent left her lips, a *no, no, no, why* of realisation. A, *they told me and I trusted you anyway.*

Gentle hands guided her to a pine, the new heavy weight of her resting against it. Her body sank back. The moulting flesh of her fingers grew into the tree, turned solid bark. Nothing to separate girl from wood anymore. Nothing to pull away from or to as she transformed just like the other girls.

Was this the pose she'd hold forever now? Not screaming or fighting, but pressed shocked and tear-stained against a tree? Another lost statue of wood and stone and moss.

Tears solidified down Kadie's cheeks, but the other girl wouldn't look at her.

"It won't hurt," she told her. But it did. She was alive, and she was dead, and she was everywhere; ash left behind from the pyre.

"It won't hurt much," Marelle corrected. Still, she wouldn't look. She used the tip of her thumbnail to scrape at a piece of tree bark.

Even burning and deadened as she was, Kadie could almost feel the scratching against her own stiffened arm. But the world around was growing dimmer, greyer. The sensation of her feet rooting through the dirt, searching, overtook her. Toes were no longer toes.

She was twisting with the roots around her, becoming less and less herself in any way she recognised. Amidst the pain, there was also the presence of all of those around her—the girls and the trees and the worms that slipped between the juncture of her roots. Less and less herself, but also more and more.

"Why?" Kadie asked. And that was that—the last word she spoke as her mouth formed a shape of accusation, and her lips turned to stone.

It echoed, strange and distant, spreading through the forest. *Why?* A pointless question that went unanswered as Marelle walked away.

♦

The fox came back to her in a dream haze, in the forest and not the forest, shifting and shimmering.

"Tried to warn you," they said.

In the dream, vines grip Kadie's flesh arms, fighting her every move. Giving no quarter; no escape.

Why, why, why?

"Tried to warn you. Now they have you—the bad men and their girl-girlie."

Kadie tried to reach out, but her fingers only twitched in response. "Help."

"Too late townie-girl," said one of the heads. "Too late, too late," said the other. "You're one of theirs now," said the first. "Just more already-dead-flesh-meat."

The fox turned double-tail and ran away with a swish. "Wait!" Kadie called. *Too late, too late.* They faded through the trees, shimmering, not-forest fading with them.

♦

The trees whisper, all of them at once. You try to find the separate threads of voice, untangle yourself from the we among them, but it's all a knot of roots. Inhale carbon dioxide, a lingering sent of petrichor. Exhale oxygen, the slow decay of radiation.

A memory of death and dying—betrayal turned to stone, mingling with lying meat-bodies who take and take and take and then leave their mess behind to soak into the earth. Your memories and not-your-memories. What's real? You. We. Everything hurts, then stops hurting and settles. Calm. Stasis. Inhale carbon dioxide, exhale oxygen, let life begin again. Is that real?

The girl comes early with her mason jars and her lies and her bad-man-stink—one of them, no better than one of them because she works for them. Who? The bad men. The burning blistered men in orange. Woodwitch, woodwitch. No such thing as a woodwitch. Just the bad men and their girl—the one who helps them steal other girls.

The lying-stealing-girl raises the lip of a jar to the cheeks of us, our newest, still trembling from the change, still unsure of what is who, what is her, what is we, we, we. Spirit drips down the edge of the jar like syrup, sap leaking out.

Our pines bristle, our hackles rise, slow and sharp. *Help.*

We want to, but what is there to do? What can we do for one human girl? One not-so-human girl? *Help.* Measure that crying in hours and minutes, here and gone before this century sets. Nothing to do but breathe.

You remember the men who wander carelessly through the forest, snapping fledgling branches and trampling beetles into the loam with heavy work boots. No amount of roaming could make them a part of the we, the forest.

The girl they call the woodwitch is theirs, and you are theirs and not theirs.

You remember being lured into the forest with sweet words and the longing that girl knew you had in you from before. You remember the other girls, Nola and Tessie and Marcie and so, so, so many others whose names you never knew. You remember their life leaching into the ground and out their pores for the bad-men to lap up.

You were there and you were not there, only the memory of a memory.

♦

A point of yellow-white light. Warning sirens. Heat and hurting and Uranium-235 racing, raging out. Flashbang of explosion. Burnt trunks laid out like a warning: *don't come any closer.* An evil mushroom rising in the air, all of you, all of us, awash in poison.

All the men and women and people dead, dead, dead. And no one telling anything, no one warning or evacuating or helping those left behind—us or them. Our bark burnt red, dying.

Regrowth. Slow, steady. Inevitable.

And then: new men in big-wheel-machines, crushing roots, running ruts through thick sediment. Coveralls and masks, didn't stop the dying, slow and ugly. But there were others to be sacrificed to their old god.

The girls.

And they took them and they drained them and they poured their spirit over the melted, twisted metal at the core of it all so the wrongness could begin again. Horror. You shrink back against it, against the knowing of it.

Easier to fade back into the we. Settle. Assimilate.

♦

Wake up, whispers the forest, a voice somehow a part of and somehow separate. A fluttering, deep inside. An aching in her chest—and there was a her, she realised. Not just a we or an us or a them, but a her. Singular. Possessive.

(Full of pain.)

Wake up, wake up, be one again, says the voice, which is really many voices, speaking as one. And it occurs to her that she's been sleeping—or something worse, very like it—and that she doesn't want to be anymore. It occurs to her that there's more than the sun and the rain and the roots of her feet.

That bad things have happened—are happening. And for the first time in maybe a long time or maybe no time at all, she becomes aware of herself again. She becomes aware of herself as herself. She had been a girl once, had had a family and a name and a cane she used to walk. Had memories and hurts all her own.

She had been Kadie. Maybe she could be again.

♦

Time passed—a lot or a little.

Kadie blinked open her eyes, which never really shut, stuck open as they were. But she became aware of them again, of seeing and sight and the forest around her. A thin frosting of ice coated the pine needles and the grey sheen of winter hung low in the air.

She was a symbiote, aware of herself, but still a part of the forest. Her roots twisted deep, twining with the trees around her. Her eyes didn't need to see with the woods watching for her. *Intruder*, the forest whispered. *Betrayer*. And there she was—Marelle.

Frost glossed the tips of her hair brittle. She made rounds, brushing fingers against the calcified skin of the other statue girls, siphoning their spirit until it dripped into the mason jars like sticky sap. Collecting them up for the men at the power plant.

Wrong wrong wrong wrong. The voice of the forest beat a heady pulse in her ears.

Marelle's fingers hesitated when they met Kadie. How many times had she done this? How many times that Kadie no longer remembered?

"I'm sorry," she said. Quiet. To herself.

And Kadie blinked—a small thing, just the shifting of eyelashes, but Marelle staggered back. The wind whipped the pine branches to a fury. *Useless words*, the needles hissed. *Pointless, lying words.*

The jars of sap slipped from her hands. Not even a gasp as they spilled—all that stolen life, gone to waste. Then she fled.

♦

Kadie was aware of time now, could count the days. Not even a full sunup to sundown before she returned, emptyhanded.

The trees bristled, wary, as Marelle approached. Some stories might say Kadie always knew she would return, but that would be too neat a lie. Kadie had no reason to trust her—even less than most—and doubted her with a fury that rivalled the oldest oaks, trembling their barren branches. The warning bark of tree frogs echoed in the clearing.

Marelle slowed, but didn't stop. She leaned in, wrapping around Kadie's stiff limbs, slotting their bodies together until they lined up. Then, ever so slowly, she pressed forward, lips to lips.

Thinking what? That whatever forest-awareness Kadie had left would soften to her? That taking this, giving it—now—would be enough?

But soft warmth spread from the touch, flowing out across Kadie's skin. Her heart stuttered in her chest—frightening, after so many days or months of stillness—like waking up again, like coming to life. Marelle's lips moved more insistently, her hands rubbing heat into Kadie's arms—not searching or seeking, but undeniably present.

"What are you doing?" Kadie asked against Marelle's lips, surprised they moved, surprised sound could slip from them at all. "How—?"

"Shhh," Marelle hushed, pressing into her body even more firmly. "I'm warming you." And "shhh," again, stopping her lips, when Kadie started to speak.

She could've stopped it—aware of the agency returned along with the movement of her eyes, lips, toes—but a part of her didn't want it to stop. The warmth was spreading along her limbs, pleasant and tingling. She hadn't even realised she was cold.

Kadie's own hands were coming back to life, fingertips questioning against the place where legs met hips met belly, unsure if it was anger or desire that drove them deep into Marelle's flesh, bruising.

They parted for breath, and Marelle held her palms out to Kadie, lit with a small amber fire that licked the air. A feral, forest instinct inside her reflexively drew back. There was question and accusation in her eyes.

Marelle said, "Hold out your hands," and placed the fire in them, encouraging, as she cupped her hands around Kadie's, who asked, "How are you doing this?"

She shook her head, unknowing, and helped guide the flame into the spot just below Kadie's collarbone where her heart should beat—used to beat and was struggling to relearn a rhythm.

She gasped. It was like instinct, this feeling. And maybe there really was such a thing as a woodwitch, because heat spread through her chest cavity, soft as honey and warm as dappled summer light. Her shoulder jerked back, slamming into the tree behind, and the hurt of it, the sharp, heady rush along her pain receptors, hit hard. Her foot twitched, and, at a thought, moved forward. Her other leg tried to follow. Before Kadie could hit the ground, Marelle caught her, limbs tangling again.

"Careful, you're only just warming up," she told her, but looking down at

Kadie's leg, they both knew that wasn't the whole truth of it.

Her good leg had thawed out, fully flesh. But the other leg—the bad one—it was still slate gray, all stiff lines of petrified wood. "Oh." She wasn't sure which one of them said it.

"It doesn't matter," said Marelle, which wasn't true, of course. It mattered as much as anything else. "I'm gonna get you out of here."

Cold wind caught against the little hairs of her arms. Winter chill. Then Marelle's words caught up with her. "Get me out of where?" Kadie asked. "Where are we going?"

"Away," she said, trying to help her walk.

But Kadie dug in, petrified leg hard against the ground. She caught Marelle's eyes with a cold look. "The other girls?"

Marelle shook her head. "I'm not even sure what it was—how I could do what I did to get you out." She skirted the words fire and magic. "I only wanted to warm you up, to undo it."

"That's not the point," said Kadie, still pulling back. "You'd leave them? After everything?" *After me,* she didn't say.

But the look on Kadie's face, reared back, must've struck her in a soft place because she wiped a hand across her eyes, and when she moved it away her look was changed with it. "They control everything here," she said. The men. She pulled down the collar of her shirt. Flesh, mottled, twisted with half-healed radiation burns. "They control me."

It crossed her mind to wonder if stone skin was the only thing that saved her from the same. Strange luck she wouldn't've needed if not for Marelle, anyway. But Kadie remembered the men from the memories—the old ones who caused the meltdown and the new ones back to start it all over again. And maybe not even whatever wild forest magic they'd tapped into was enough to stand against it.

"Their cure—it's the only thing keeping me alive," she said, almost a plea, like knowing this might make up for what she did in Kadie's mind, like her life was equal to the damage she'd done.

But Kadie wasn't the only one it'd been done to. And she could still feel the warmth glowing from just under her collarbone. She considered the copse of stone girls frosted over around her. "So we'll just have to take it back."

◆

Her joints were stiffer than they had been, still unlearning their stone rigor. Walking was slow and painful, every step an agony. Her cane was lost, but Marelle offered up an arm, wrapping the other around Kadie's waist. Her leg dragged a rut into the muddy ground behind them.

They were racing against borrowed time. She could feel the anxious energy of the trees around her, the soft *turn around, go back* as the wind whistled the tips of barren branches. The fox ran alongside them, veering out of the brush to fall in step. For once silent, nothing clever to say.

A dried-up creek bed demarked the edge of the living forest, almost normal but for the silence. No branches rustling, no insects buzzing, just unsettling quiet where it shouldn't be. Like everything knew to steer clear. Marelle's hand tightened around Kadie's waist.

The two-headed fox skidded to a halt at the bank. *Foolish girl-girlies*, they growled, almost sadly, as Kadie and Marelle crossed over, ankle deep in mud. Burnt up trunks all that was left beyond the far bank. The border to the outermost edge of the explosion.

They skirted concentric circles of felled trees, stopped at the rotting door of an old fallout shelter dug into the ground—much good it did anyone. Marelle prized it open, disappearing inside. Kadie could only peer down after her. Something white and skeletal glinted from the corner, and she suppressed a shiver.

Rations lined the shelves, mason jars full of apples and peaches and okra and the like. Bags of rice too, probably wormy now. Had Marelle lived here? She traced her fingers along the jars, searching, until she pulled two vials of something milky, climbed back out.

There were gaps in Kadie's not-memories, the thoughts she'd inherited from the trees. "You work for them," she said.

"I told you—"

"But why *you*?" A regular girl. A town girl.

"Why any of us?" Marelle responded, then seemed to acknowledge that that wasn't enough. Not even close to what she was looking for. "They needed bodies and thought I might make one of them at first. But they'd had trouble over the years—getting the girls. A group of unfamiliar men? Now, that's suspicious. But I'm not." And then: "You went easily enough, didn't you?"

Kadie didn't have anything to say to that.

Marelle uncapped a syringe. "Last chance," she told Kadie, pulling white fluid up into the glass cylinder. "You can still leave. Run away. Never look back." So quietly, under her breath, that Kadie almost didn't hear it: "Not let them get to you like I did."

Kadie ignored all of that, said instead, "What is it?"

"An antidote. A way out," said Marelle. A precious few vials Marelle must've stolen over the years, hoarded, maybe in the hopes of escaping one day. She offered it up, and Kadie wondered if that small dose would be enough to save her, too? Or only delay the inevitable?

And maybe it would've ended like that, a tidy little tale with the girls conquering the rumours of the woodwitch, surviving the irradiated forest and saving themselves to live happily ever after in some little cottage by a stream in the woods. You could stop here and believe they did.

But the full truth, if you want it, is this: Kadie wrapped her hand around the syringe. "Or a way forward," she said, and Marelle nodded. That too.

Marelle demonstrated how to depress the plunger, inject the fluid into the vein. Explained how it would give them time—a bit of it anyway—to go deeper into the wreckage, to reach the old power plant where the men who used her still worked and lived. And so they went.

The burnt black edges of the power plant rose in the distance, no trees to obscure it. And Kadie could see them from a distance, the men in bulky protective suits rebuilding the walls, scrubbing away the contamination. One of them turned, and even under the mask she could see the way his skin peeled back at the edges, scabs, red-brown and bloody.

Marelle pushed her down behind a pile of rubbish—old trash and scrap the people in town might've been able to find a use for. She told her not to go any further, that the antidote did only so much. That the rest was up to her.

Marelle approached the orange-suited men with ease, face exposed, hair tangled. She spoke words Kadie couldn't hear. Annoyed faces. Arms waving. He grabbed her roughly by the shoulder. A breathless moment on the precipice of all being lost.

And then.

The reason Marelle'd wanted to approach alone—the real reason, or one of them, anyway. She pulled a sealed jar from under her coat, not full of okra or apples or beets or anything at all she ought to've had. Full of something sticky— like sap. And Kadie didn't need to hear the trees to know.

Taker. Liar. Traitor. Thief.

The trees had warned her, hadn't they? The fox, too.

The men gathered around the jar, joking, laughing. Sharp, sour bile rose in Kadie's throat as they grabbed it in meaty hands. Marelle followed them to the door, face a blank mask. She watched them take the jar into the plant, to pour over the reactor, to put some stolen life back into it. Kadie felt sick.

But then Marelle shut the door, all the men trapped behind it. She grabbed some scrap to lodge against the handle, using her own weight to help hold it shut. It wouldn't be enough.

Kadie could hear the seedlings of the wrecked forest around her—just starting to grow back—with their strange babbling in the distance. Unintelligible. Unsettling. It wasn't too late for them. She ran as fast as her bad leg would let her, scraping through the mud and debris until she was leaning back alongside Marelle, bracing against the door. The men hadn't even realised yet, hadn't started pounding. They would. Their suits would only last so long that close to the melted core.

Marelle spoke something that she perhaps thought was an apology: "I had to give them something," she said, "for them to let me get close."

Pricks like tiny needles spread across her skin. The door felt hot to the touch. Too much radiation, too close. Her dosimeter would've been screaming, but she didn't need it to know what the sharp stinging all across her arms and neck and head meant.

Marelle had wanted to end this once and for all, entomb the men with their reactor where none of them could do any more harm. Maybe she was willing to die for that, since she was certainly dying already, but Kadie wasn't.

The amber glow of sunset illuminated the tangle of veins in her own chest. And if she could put fire in, well, it wasn't so different to take it back out, was it? That instinct again: she reached in, plucking a strand of flames from her chest, hoping she wasn't taking too much, hoping it was enough. Marelle backed away as Kadie cupped the flame against the seal of the door, warping it into one sheet of solid, white-hot metal.

Marelle just looked at her, wide-eyed in shock. And Kadie was almost as surprised it had worked. But it had, and even still breathing heavy, she had to believe it was enough.

"There," she said. "It's done."

♦

They walked back across the dry creek, past the old fallout shelter, through a welcoming murmur from the trees—the only others who knew what they'd done. And, well, it's obvious, isn't it—what would happen next?

Shouting and the gold glisten of flashlights in the distance. They called her name—"Kadie! Kadie!" A search party. A hunting party. Looking through the woods for months now, maybe. Ever since Kadie disappeared. One final girl—enough to force them out, to finally get them looking.

They both registered the shouting, carrying around the narrow trunks, the pitch and timber of their nearing search. Kadie started toward them, fast as her stiffened leg would carry her.

But Marelle held back. Kadie turned to look at her, questioning squint to her eyes. "They think I'm the woodwitch," said Marelle, and wasn't it something Kadie knew from the start? *Unnatural*, they'd said. *Brain-muddled* and *untrustworthy* and *there'll be a new one missing soon, ya hear?*

Well, now they'd found her, their woodwitch.

It didn't matter if the stories weren't true; she'd lured Kadie away, hadn't she?

Kadie bit her lip. Her time in the forest hadn't left her unchanged either. The pins and needles sting was gone from her skin, but the blisters remained. How much good could the antidote do against that? She could stay, too, live a life out here before the cancer got her, where no one would question the grey of her leg or the soft glow of her chest through her shirt.

But Marelle wasn't the only girl who needed saving.

"Go," Marelle urged her, handing back the bag she'd thought she'd lost all those days (or months or years) ago. The meaning behind the word implicit: telling Kadie to leave her behind. Maybe a part of one or the other thought she deserved it anyway.

Kadie looked back, just once. Marelle's lips were tinged cold-gray in the winter air. Her eyelashes tipped in frost that flaked off with every blink. All her apologies unsaid. "Go."

And she did. The whispers of the forest followed her, long after she'd led the search party back to the other girls. After she showed them how to rub the warmth back into their stony skin, after they wrapped them in blankets and led them back to town, after she waved off their questions and pretended not to hear their words, in pitying undertones, forgiving her reticence because of the 'poor girl's time with that woodwitch' ("Did you see her? Awful, awful, and those burns"). After, she unpacked her bag, placed the book and compass and jagged chunk of quartz on her windowsill and stared out for an uncountable number of minutes.

WHERE ELSE BUT QUEENSLAND

Paradox Delilah

Featured in Issue #80

EWALDINE "EWIE" ENDERS WAS uncomfortable, unimpressed, and shit out of luck. She was uncomfortable because the climate in far North Queensland, Australia, was so humid that the thick, sticky air was not only causing her outer human skin to sweat, but also leaking through to her natural, scaled skin underneath. The subsequent chafing made her entire body feel as papery as her tongue, when she'd had the misfortune of drinking over-brewed tea. She was unimpressed because the tourists surrounding her on the crocodile spotting cruise were too busy prattling about the sights they'd already seen on their travels to immerse themselves in the beauty of the Daintree River surrounding them. Their voices grated on Ewie's sensitive ears, and their ignorance felt like a reflection of her idiocy for embarking on this quest. To quote the colourful language of the locals, she was shit out of luck, because to reach her destination, she was going to have to jump from the safety of the boat and into the crocodile-infested waters below.

Ewie had been of two minds about whether or not she wanted to spot crocodiles. On the one hand, it would be interesting to see one of the great creatures that shared the blood of her ancestors. On the other hand, this species had missed the great evolution and were unaware of her species' existence. They wouldn't see her as any different from the noisy, tasty humans aboard the boat. So she'd decided—when it became time to begin her mission and swim through the crocodile-infested waters to her destination—she'd rather there not be a crocodile lying in wait for her. Their jaws could snap down upon prey with a force even Ewie's scaled skin could not withstand.

"Oh you beauty, would you have a look at that. We've got a big'n over here to our right."

Everyone swivelled to the right, scanning the water and the mud banks flanking the river. Ewie's eyes landed on the crocodile first, homing in on the heat signal of the creature's body. When her eyes readjusted to optical vision, she was filled with awe. The crocodile was nearly fifteen feet long, its heavily armoured torso blending into the muted browns of the riverbank. Even from the protection of the boat, the crocodile felt too close. There was a primeval edge to its form, unmoved by the presence of the gawking tourists. Hundreds of shutters snapped, as amateur photographers vied for the perfect holiday snap. With each click, Ewie felt her body—the real one, underneath—clam up, the mucus membranes inside her throat clenching with unease.

This was a really dumb idea. *Save the planet. Become a hero. Be forgiven by the Holy Trinidad.* Who was she kidding? Ewie didn't give a hoot about this planet or the moronic bipeds that called it home. Let their planet be destroyed and taken over by a villainous race. Was all this really worth the risk to her own being?

The boat skipper radioed to the other boats in the company, alerting them to the presence of the fifteen-footer, and then steered Ewie's boat further south along the river. Despite the heat, the sky was wrapped in a sheath of dark grey clouds, and was growing darker by the minute. The darker the sky grew, the more insidious the humidity felt against Ewie's outer skin. Beads of perspiration felt like a swarm of insects crawling across her back. With a warning call of two solitary splats on the boat's tin roof, a downpour started, hitting hard against the river surface all around them. The skipper abandoned his post at the helm and lumbered down the central walkway to the front of the boat. He pulled on some cables, and a flimsy shield of plastic descended in front of the people in the first row.

"It'll help a little, but a rainforest *is* called a rainforest for a reason."

He offered a smirk, pleased at his own wit. The tourists around him nodded meekly, though the rain still slashed at them from the boat's sides. Those seated on the outer edges started to squeeze past those on the aisle seats, opting to stand rather than become further drenched. Ewie was the only one who stayed seated in the rain. The skipper had lost the attention of most of the tourists, but still continued his narration.

"Now this collection of trees to the right is actually a small island. We're going to follow the river bend around it until we get back to the main river. Funny story about this island is it's actually home to some wild pigs that some galah introduced back in the day. The bloody things had to swim across this croc-infested river to get to it, but the buggers managed somehow, and it's their home now."

Ewie gulped. This was it. Her point of no return. She shifted her gaze around to check out the crowd on the boat. No one was looking in her direction. The skipper was doing his best to search for crocodiles on the other bank, whilst craning his neck past the drenched bodies blocking his views. Searching the water, Ewie couldn't detect any sizeable heat signals, but that didn't mean there weren't any crocs nearby. She checked the mud flats and mangroves flanking the island, but couldn't detect any movement or life. There was only rain, and the deep fear in the pit of her second stomach. Her centre of gravity was attempting to anchor itself to the seat beneath her. She had to fight back.

Ewie leapt up, shooting a final glance at the skipper before flinging herself off the boat and into the murky depths below. The flat sheet of water broke against her hands and face like a plate of glass, piercing and bursting all around her. As soon as the initial splash settled down, she felt unmistakable ripples in the water heading her way. A large shape, agile but powerful. She began swimming, her arms executing the rhythmic but maladroit stroke humans relied upon for speed. Her senses were overwhelmed with motions and noise, but she was aware of shouting from the boat, reaching her ears in bursts between the walls of rain.

"Someone's in the water."

"Woman overboard."

"Croc! Croc!"

"It's going to get her."

"Swim faster, mate. Swim faster."

She was twelve feet away from the mangroves that lined the edge of the island when she felt the large presence catching up to her. It was nearly on her, and in her human skin she wouldn't be able to outpace it. She needed a new plan. She needed...

A life preserver?

One of the dolts on the boat had thrown one at her, the orange ring landing with a thwack against the water directly in front of her face. She grabbed it with her hands, opening her human mouth wide enough to expose the decidedly inhuman canines waiting beneath. She sunk eight of these teeth into the preserver, bursting the thick plastic and deflating the ring with frenetic energy. She compressed it into a round, hard object, and when the jaws of the beast below opened up to seize her, she shoved the thick bundle of plastic deep into the back of the creature's mouth.

The crocodile recoiled instantly, fighting against the wedged hazard in its throat. Ewie dove deep into the murky water beneath it, and swam through the darkness to the mangrove roots beyond. Closing her eyes and focusing on the currents and density of the water, Ewie could envision the landscape surrounding her. The presence of the mangrove roots alerted her when to swim upwards, where she emerged six feet into the camouflage of the island. She rested, her back lying on some craggy roots. She wasn't relaxed; her heart was still pounding triple its normal speed.

"What are you doing here, sis?"

Ewie shot up, her eyes racing to find the source of the voice. She saw the clothing first—bright orange board shorts, lime green and white striped tank, all dry—and then she found the young man's face, dark brown skin and hair, camouflaged against the trunk of a tree.

"That was a pretty stupid move you pulled there. You been watching too many Steve Irwin TV shows out there in space?"

"Not sure who that is—or what you mean." Ewie looked around, "Do you live here?"

"Ha. This island's not fit for human living."

"...then what are you doing here?"

The man raised his eyebrows at Ewie in amusement. "I'm trying to figure out what in the hell you're up to. I saw you this morning. That was my people's land you appeared on out of nowhere. It's my people's land you're still on now."

Ewie didn't make a move, cautiously appraising the man.

"It really confused the local birds, you know. A big empty space they couldn't fly through. Confused the hell out of me watching them, too. Then you popped out, all secretive like. Just had to follow you and see what was up. And then you came here, of all places. What's a—what, *interstellar*—traveller doing going on a croc cruise? And jumping off the boat, like a true idiot? You better not be trophy hunting."

"I, uh—" Ewie noticed the long stick resting in the young man's left hand, the rock ground to a sharp point at its tip. "Is that a weapon?"

The man smiled. "Yep. Your regular, everyday spear. Normally, it just decorates our living room with Dad's other Bama stuff, but I figured it might have a more practical use today. And yeah, I know how to use it. I learnt when I was a kid."

Ewie nodded.

"Okay. I'm not, trophy hunting, whatever that is. I'm here to save your stinking planet."

"Right."

"Seriously. There's this ancient species, the Wurrumbini, they hid a device here thousands of years ago. It's been terraforming your planet one millionth of a degree at a time. Once the climate's warm enough, it'll be fit for them to live here, and also inhospitable for humans. So, I'm here to disarm the device."

"Yeah, and I'm Father Fucking Christmas."

"I don't know what that is."

"It's like the story you're telling right now. Just some bullshit made up by a white fella. Well, in this case, sheila."

"I really wish it was. But all the inexplicable weather events, extreme temperatures, flooding, freak storms your planet is suffering from—they're side effects of the terraforming, and it's only going to get worse. So you should be afraid, and also very grateful, because I'm going to go battle the guardians of the device, destroy it, and save you all."

She watched as the young man considered her words, before puffing out his chest and grinning.

"Nah sis, you should be thankful to me. You're in no condition to go battle anyone, and you're unarmed. I'll come with. We can save this stinking planet together. I'm Jiemba."

"Jim-ba? I'm Ewaldine—Ewie. But thanks, I don't need a man to help me. I can handle this on my own."

Jiemba smiled at Ewie. "Sure you can, sis. Just in case you're wrong though, maybe you should look down at your arm before you go wandering off on your own."

"I don't know what you're…"

Ewie couldn't finish her sentence once she'd glanced to where her left arm should have been located. Where her shirt sleeve ended, so did her arm. Goopy strands of skin and flesh hung limply for an inch or two before abruptly ending. Underneath these unfortunate dregs, her natural arm was also severed. Her scales had been ripped apart, the pasty white flesh beneath oozing an insipid yellow goo. As soon as she saw it, she felt it. Screams of pain from her missing limb. She clutched at the stump with her right hand, mentally cursing before relaxing her grip and searching inside her drenched waist belt for a small vial of healing cream.

"Could you?"

She held out the vial to Jiemba, who eyed her curiously before opening it and passing it back. Ewie dumped the cream onto her stump, dropping the container so her hand could be free to rub the cream in. She watched as it sealed the open wounds shut, like a flame cauterising a wound.

"Well that's handy," Jiemba said, before pointing to the vial. "You'll be wanting to take that canister back with you. No point trashing the place you're trying to save."

Self-conscious, Ewie nodded, pocketing the empty vial back into her belt. She offered a cautious smile to Jiemba.

"I think I will accept your offer to help."

"No problem. It is my planet, after all. So which way are we heading?"

"To the island centre. Would you mind helping me up?"

Errant branches and slippery roots writhed in every direction before them as they walked, slowing their progress to the island's centre. With Ewie's arm missing, her gait was off kilter, but Jiemba moved with a faultless ease and was able to assist her. He would calculate when Ewie would need assistance before Ewie was even aware herself.

"How far did you come to get here?"

"Well, I hadn't decided to come here until I'd already been running for a year, but I guess you could call it, maybe two years."

"Fark, that's a long way. What were ya running from?"

"My own idiocy... I upset some really powerful people. But it's okay. I'll save your planet and then all will be forgiven."

Ewie's face contorted as she considered if she'd actually be welcomed home. She doubted anyone would be ecstatic, but if she got the Holy Trinidad on her side, they'd have to at least let her back in.

"Hey look," Jiemba said, gesturing ahead of them, "Wild pig."

Ewie scanned the tree line, switching to heat vision when she couldn't see the pig through the swath of vines. Jiemba was right. A small one, muddy brown skin, searching the ground for treats.

"How'd you see that?"

"It's easy to see things when you're not stuck inside your own head. That and it's making as much noise with its snout as you are with your feet. Can you walk any louder?"

Ewie felt her ears go red with embarrassment.

"Sorry, I'm...this isn't really my forte. I'm more of a swimmer."

"Wet planet then, your home?"

"Yes."

"Cool."

Ewie coughed, trying to deepen her voice and add an authoritative edge.

"So that pig, we've got to follow it back to its den. The pigs on this island are the guardians of the device."

Jiemba stopped dead in his tracks, turning to stare sceptically at Ewie.

"The pigs? What have they got to benefit from this? They're pigs!"

"They're not, actually. They're low level cretins who've been transmuted to resemble pigs. They're probably going to try kill us when they notice us, too. So let's let stop talking and return to tracking, okay?"

They walked in silence, following the pig from a distance. It seemed unaware of their presence, and stopped frequently to munch on hidden delights buried in the dirt. The trunks of grey and stifled brown grew denser, and strangler fig vines lashed nearby trees and fallen limbs together, their weaving filtering out of the remnants of sun. Birds—lorikeets—were screeching above them, greeting each other as they settled into trees for the night. In the distance, hundreds of wings flapped as fruit bats began to wake up. Mosquitos began to buzz around them, but detoured with haste when they caught Ewie's scent. Jiemba began to meld into the darkness as night fell, only the vividness of his tank and shorts belying his presence.

"How'd you manage to follow me all day when you're wearing such bright, garish colours?" Ewie said.

"Sometimes when you're not expecting to see things, you just don't, sis. And they're not garish, they're happy, and they look great with my skin tone."

Ewie smiled to herself, comforted by Jiemba's quiet swagger. He was a good companion. Astute, observant, and with the confidence of someone who always knew what he was doing. Ewie was lacking all those characteristics. She spoke too much, too often, and rarely knew what she was doing until it was over. Like now. She had no idea what the fuck they would do once they arrived at the pig's lair. Die, probably. Best not to mention that to Jiemba.

The dense foliage overhead had been sheltering them from the rain, but the trees began thinning and the rain began hurtling down upon them like hundreds of rocks on a tin roof. Ewie was used to being immersed in water, but she didn't like this new arrangement where it thrashed atop her head. She cast a side eye at Jiemba, but before she could speak, someone else did.

One of the pigs.

It was right in front of them, its dark hide covered in mud, the whites of its eyes reflecting what shards of moonlight reached down here. And it wasn't the only one. Nearly twenty sets of eye whites glinted around them.

"What are you doing here, Gatta Kimbala?"

The pig's voice was low and threatening, its English stilted. Ewie improvised, bowing down to politely bob before its face.

"Your masters of the Wurrumbini have sent me here to check on the planet changer and ensure it is still working properly." She smiled, shrugging her shoulders. "I'm the maintenance woman."

The pig raised its head higher, lifting its upper torso to stand on its hind legs. All of the other pigs in the clearing mimicked the action.

"Maintenance woman? We have been guarding this device for 50,000 years. Not once have the Wurrumbini questioned our ability to perform our duty."

"Yes, but protecting is a bit different to checking function, and you don't exactly have the digits to perform that task." She wiggled her fingers at them. "And between you and me, you're a bit isolated down here, and there has actually been some talk up there in regards to the quality of your work..."

The pig baulked. "The quality of our work? How dare you."

Its torso bobbed angrily above its legs, swaying unsteadily.

Ewie started talking faster.

"Look, those aren't my opinions. I'm just the maintenance woman. But if you allow me to do my job and look at the device, I'll be able to report back that you're doing an exemplary job."

The pig began to calm, but then switched its focus to Jiemba.

"This is one of the local inhabitants of this planet, he should not be here. His people caused the Wurrumbini much ire when they first came here. We should eat him."

"No, eating him is definitely a bad idea. He's my guide on and off this island. He cannot be disposed of until I have been safely seen back to my ship."

"What?"

Ewie turned to Jiemba, holding a hand up to quiet him. "Know your place, human, and accept your purpose."

Jiemba narrowed his eyes at Ewie, but then nodded, a gesture that seemed to qualm the pig's reservations.

"We'll take you to the planet changer, Gatta Kimbala. This way."

The pigs all slid back onto their front legs, and moved deeper into the forest together. They trotted in sync with one another, their large bellies swinging in unison. Ewie and Jiemba had to take large strides to keep pace with them, and if they began to lag, an overzealous pig behind them would headbutt their legs to speed them up. The rain receded again, trapped in the foliage above them, but the ground was thick and muddy. The pigs ahead of them began to close ranks, focused in on a single point: a dense circle of giant forest trees, tightly wrapped in barbed fig vines. There was only one small opening, large enough for a single pig to fit through. Ewie and Jiemba's entourage parted ahead of them, and the leader pig gestured for them to step through.

"We'll be watching you, maintenance woman."

Ewie nodded, but kept her gaze forward. Inside the circle, the deep greens of the rainforest were replaced with muted browns, the giant forest trees dead and hollow. The ground was a depressed layer of dirt, and half-buried in its centre, was a black object similar in size and shape to an ostrich egg. There appeared to be a thin line of haze in the air, rising from a small hole in the dome of the device, extending up into the sky.

"That's it?" Jiemba said, "That's the planet changer? I thought it would be more impressive. It looks like an incense diffuser."

"Do incense diffusers shoot out harmonic phase pulses into the ionosphere? Because that's what that thing's doing."

"Right... So what happens now? You just punch in some code and it deactivates?"

"Ssh!" Ewie gestured for Jiemba to quiet, checking the heat sources of the pigs on the other side of the thicket. When she was satisfied they hadn't heard anything compromising, she whispered to Jiemba. "I don't think there is a code. I think we might just have to try to disassemble it."

Jiemba took a long, drawn-out breath.

"Think? Are you just winging this?"

"Maybe."

"For the love of Bama. We're surrounded by talking pigs with murderous intentions and you don't even have a plan?"

"Yes."

"Fark." Jiemba shook his head at her. "I'd be lying if I said this wasn't extremely frustrating. And stressful. But okay then. Let's come up with a plan and save my stinking planet."

"Great."

Jiemba narrowed his eyes at her, "Yeah, nah. Definitely *not* great."

Ewie smiled, and turned her back before Jiemba could protest more. She fixed her attention on the device. There were three ridges in its surface, intricate lines spanning its six-inch circumference. Careful to keep her face away from the device's dome, Ewie crouched down to trace the lines, searching for an access point to the device's interior.

"Shoot."

"What?"

"I have no idea how to open this up. I studied Wurrumbini technology in school, but obviously their weapons of mass destruction weren't on the syllabus. We need to open it to disable it. I don't know how to. Thoughts?"

"Could we smash it open?"

"Without drawing the attention of the pigs? Nope. They'd hear it before we were successful."

Jiemba nodded at the line of hazy air.

"What about that? You said that's what's causing all the problems, right sis? Can we direct it back onto itself? Reflect it or something?"

"That's ridiculous."

"Is it?"

Ewie thought for a moment. "No, actually, that might work. I don't know what we'd use though. Do you have a mirror hidden under your tank top?"

"Nah. I have tweezers in my pocket, though."

"Tweezers? What are they going to do?"

Jiemba paused for a moment, pretending to appraise Ewie.

"Well, you're probably not going to like this, sis. But...those scales of yours, what are they made from? They look very strong...and some might say, reflective..."

Ewie looked down at her cauterised stump, and the scales protruding out from underneath the tatters of human skin.

"Don't. Even. Think. About. It."

"Come on. I'm guessing you've got hundreds of scales underneath there. Are you really going to miss *one*?"

"One? I lost an entire arm today already."

"Yeah, but it'll grow back, right? You're like some kind of lizard-alien? Lizards grow back their tails all the time."

It was Ewie's turn to take a long, drawn out breath, but because she was trying not to lose her shit, *not* for dramatic affect.

"I am *not* a lizard, and arms *do not* just grow back. I'm going to be good ol' one-armed Ewie for the rest of my life now."

"Right. But is one more scale really going to be the straw that broke the camel's back?"

"Camel?"

"Yeah, a big animal with two bumps on its back. They store a lot of water in—"

Jiemba stopped talking, his eyes widened and he pointed to the thicket behind Ewie. Ewie mouthed at him, "What?" before turning to look herself.

And then she shrieked in pain.

"Owwwwww."

She whipped her body back around to see Jiemba victoriously waving one of her scales back at her, in the grasp of the tweezer prongs.

"See, no big deal. Now if we just—" He stopped, cocking his head to the side. "Can you hear that?"

"Yeah, I'm not falling for that again."

"No seriously. Is that…chanting?"

They both listened this time. The pigs were grunting. Not normal, communicative grunts. Low and rhythmic ones, in unison. Ewie's face paled.

"That's a war chant. They're getting ready for battle."

"You think they figured out you're not a maintenance woman?"

"Yeah. They must have a way to contact the Wurrumbini. I thought they were isolated out here."

"Do you have an exit strategy?"

Ewie reached inside her waist satchel, and pulled out a small stone.

"My ship can beam us back in. But we have to disable the device first."

"Right. Well you distract the pigs, and I'll destroy this bugger."

Jiemba switched his attention back to the device, reaching his scale-wielding tweezer hand forward. Outside the thicket, the chanting was growing louder. Ewie recovered a small jar of blue powder from her satchel, and started sprinkling it in a circle around the two of them and the device. Jiemba held the scale at level with the device opening, ready to slide it across. His fingers were starting to shake from proximity to the harmonic waves, but he held his tweezer hand steady with his left hand. With a silent prayer to no particular god, he manoeuvred the thick, black scale across the opening. The air above immediately settled, but the scale began to vibrate. It took all of Jiemba's strength to hold it steady.

The trees shook around them as the pigs charged at the thicket. Three pigs made it through the opening, tusked mouths gnashing as they rushed at Ewie and Jiemba. Ewie shrieked, even as she shoved her forefingers into her mouth and threw a gob of spit onto the blue powder. It ignited upon impact, and then blue flames lashed around them in a protective circle. The pigs cried in outrage, and even the ever-confident Jiemba swore in shock.

"Think you could hurry that up?" Ewie shouted over the noise of the flames, and the pigs' chanting, "This fire is only going to hold for a few minutes!"

"Then why didn't you make a better fire? Use my spear."

Ewie nodded and picked up the spear, bouncing it once in her hand to feel its weight. She stood poised, watching as the pigs thrashed against the blue flames, hoping to get in.

In Jiemba's hand, the tweezers and the scale were quivering. Beads of sweat began to form on Jiemba's hands as he pushed the scale down, sealing the device opening. When he did, actual steam began to seep out from underneath the scale.

"Sis, it's steaming. That's a good sign, right? Tell me it's a good sign."

Ewie had her back turned to Jiemba.

"Kinda busy here!" Ewie shouted, as the blue flames disappeared and a pig lunged towards her.

She stabbed at the pig, but her blow was weak without her second arm to help it. The pig came at her again, and again she flailed the spear in its direction.

The two other pigs launched at Jiemba. He kicked at the closest one, and it flew back into its companion. The momentum knocked Jiemba off balance, and his hands lost their position above the sky changer. The device's opening was fully exposed.

But there was no haze.

Only steam.

And creaking.

So loud it sounded like a giant tree about to uproot.

And uproot it did.

With a crack as loud as lightning, the device split open, steam erupting all over the thicket. A wave of air pressure exploded above their heads, ricocheting up the circle of tree trunks until finally dissipating into the canopy. Branches came crashing down upon them, one landing on the two pigs attacking Jiemba, another where Ewie's left arm should have been.

"Yikes."

Ewie shot Jiemba a frantic look, and in unison the two of them began sprinting away from base of destruction. Four pigs gave chase, but the rest remained behind, mourning the loss of the device. The pursuit pigs moved fast, clipping at their heels. A tusk grazed against Jiemba's left calf, bruising the skin. He started hop-running, to keep his long legs above the pigs' head height as much as possible.

He shouted over to Ewie, "How long 'til you can activate your ship-beaming thing?"

"Well that's the thing—" Ewie shouted between breaths and strides, "It'll actually only work for one of us."

Jiemba nearly stopped dead in his tracks, but was reminded not to by the loud growl of a pig behind him.

"You cannot be serious right now, sis."

"I know, I know, it's kind of awful, but it didn't feel right to bring it up earlier... I have a plan though."

"Oh yeah, leave me behind?"

"No no, I'll run with you as far as the water, distract the pigs, and then when you're safe on the river I'll beam myself away."

"You think those pigs are afraid of the crocs?"

"Of course, everyone's afraid of saltwater crocodiles."

"And me? You think the crocs don't eat locals?"

"No," Ewie shouted, struggling hard to project over the rain and the efforts of their running, "But I did notice your shorts were dry this morning, so I'm guessing you have a boat somewhere."

"You're not as unobservant as I first thought, my strange alien friend."

Ewie couldn't believe how Jiemba managed to sound condescending whilst shouting and running away from killer pigs.

"Alright Jiemba, now's the time for your final mile. I'll keep them busy over here while you get away."

"You sure you're gonna be okay, sis?"

"Of course, and why do you keep calling me 'sis?' We're not vaguely related."

"Yeah, nah." Jiemba shouted over his shoulder, "But I forgot your name pretty much as soon as you said it to me, and it never felt like the right time to bring it up. See you next time you're on Earth, space woman!"

Ewie chuckled as Jiemba raced away from her, nearing the island's edge. Ewie circled back, shouting at the four pigs.

"Come here, you big swine. I can't believe you fell for that maintenance woman act."

They growled, chasing her down, each aiming to skewer her on their tusks. Ewie doubled back, further away from Jiemba and the island's edge, and then worked on distancing herself from the pigs behind her. She was making headway, until she paused to check Jiemba had made it onto the safety of the river. It was hard to see him in the darkness, so she had to use her thermal vision. She located him safe on the river, but she'd miscalculated how far the lead pig was. In her moment of distraction, it lunged from the bushes beside her and sunk its jaw around her right arm.

She screamed, shaking her arm left and right. The pig didn't fly off, and its three cohorts, inspired by their companion's success, were picking up speed towards them, eager to join the attack. Ewie gritted her teeth, shaking her whole torso to loosen the pig's grasp. Again it didn't work, so she opened her jaw wide, dislocating the human mouth piece and allowing her natural canines to protrude out. She bit down, hard, tearing at the skin below her right shoulder. As it tore apart, the motion of the shaking and the weight of the pig's body caused the skin to peel back down her arm, like a thick tube of pink rubber, covered on the underside with an elasticised brine. The pig's hold on her arm slid, and Ewie was able to pull her true, scaled arm free of the mess.

Ewie began sprinting again, tearing at the skin suit still covering her torso as she ran. The pigs behind her lunged at the pieces that came flying back at them, at first not understanding the meaning of the errant pieces of flesh and clothes. Most of Ewie's upper body was now exposed, an armour of brine covered scales, strong black diamonds with relics of human flesh caught between their spines. Near her collarbone, the scales rapidly changed in colour to a light blue, leading up to her neck. The human mask still sat on Ewie's head, flopping in a haphazard manner as she took large strides away from the pigs. She wanted to rip the mask off—it was irritating, and suffocating, and about as much as she could stand—but she knew there was a more important task at hand.

She had to activate the ship's recall control, before the pigs caught up.

She fumbled in her waist pouch, procuring the stone.

She had done what she had come for.

Save the planet. Become a hero. Be forgiven by the Holy Trinidad.

But the stone didn't work.

Instead of being teleported to her ship's forward deck, she was thrown face first, screaming, into the muddy ground.

"Ack." Ewie spit out a mouthful of dirt, as her torso was pressed to the ground by two hooves stepping onto her back. The four pigs had caught up with her.

Their leader spoke, "There will be no escape for you, Gatta Kimbala. Only death."

"Ooof," Ewie managed, forcing her vocal chords to work despite the absence of air in her lungs. "Does it really have to be death? Couldn't we settle for torture, or maybe you could hand me over to the Wurrumbini?"

The pig on her left cried with outrage, the one atop of her stamped its forward hooves down harder.

Ewie squeaked, "That's a no, then?"

The pig atop her leaned down so their faces were level, and pierced the human skin on her face with its tusk. It growled, "That's a no," and then whipped its head to the right, tearing Ewie's face open with its tusk. Patches of bright, deep blue scales shone through from under the gelatinous remnants of human flesh. All four pigs were silenced by the sight, trying to remember the significance of the darker blue scales.

"You're—" The largest of the pigs began to speak, but was stopped by a shotgun blast exploding its torso.

A deep, male voice yelled out, "Oi. Piss off, you filthy buggers."

The remaining three pigs scattered before their companion's body had even toppled to the ground.

"You alright there, love? I always thought it was bloody stupid introducing pigs to this country."

The boat skipper appeared in Ewie's periphery, reaching down to help her up. He paused when he registered her mangled face, missing arm, and scaled skin.

"Bloody hell, this doesn't seem normal."

He leaned back, mouth agape, staring for a solid three minutes. He slapped his own face a couple of times, to check he wasn't imagining things.

"No offence, I mean…I'm happy to help you and please, still give us a 5 Star Yelp review, but…do you know what a Yelp review is?"

Ewie shook her head, and then flinched from the pain.

"Right." The skipper held a stoic expression on his face, forcing himself to remain calm. "Well, if I return to base missing a passenger again, it's not going to be pretty. We can cover you in a poncho, no one needs to see what you are. And then do you have any friends who can come get ya, or should I be calling our local ambulance services?" He lifted Ewie up, one arm under her scaled shoulders, another under her legs, where scales peeked through the holes of torn human flesh. "Or is it the vet from the reptile zoo up the road I should be calling?"

Before Ewie could respond, a sharp spear head appeared at the back of the skipper's neck. Jiemba's face materialised behind it.

"You don't want to be calling anyone, brother. I can take her from here."

"Look mate, I'm sure you can, but we have a duty of care to all our passengers to make sure they return to the dock safely after one of our tours, human or not."

Jiemba pressed the spear a little harder into the skipper's neck.

"I'm afraid this is non-negotiable. Ewie is coming with me."

Ewie said, "I thought you forgot my name."

Jiemba smiled, "It came back to me, right around the time I heard you scream in the distance and realised I wanted to know you were okay.

"Look uh," The skipper leant his neck forward, away from the spear point, so that he could turn around to face Jiemba. "I don't want to cause any problems, but I really have to take this sheila back to the dock or legal will shut us down. Two disappearances in two years is too many. Why don't you come back with me, and after the headcount, you can go wherever you want? Please?"

Ewie nodded her acceptance, so Jiemba shrugged. "Sure."

The skipper carried Ewie back to the tour boat, where a throng of tourists waited. Half were concerned for the missing passenger's well-being, the other half concerned that they might miss their connecting tours. Collectively they craned their necks to get a better view of Ewie from underneath her hooded poncho, but they all obeyed when the skipper demanded they turn off their cameras and phones.

Jiemba sat beside Ewie on the trip back to shore, his canoe trailing behind them on a rope. She watched the moonlight dance across his dark skin and said, "I can't believe you came back for me."

Jiemba said, "I can't believe you went into that situation with zero plan and succeeded."

Ewie smiled, "Well, I had some help."

"Some? Yeah, nah. I saved your scaled butt from certain failure."

"I guess that's true. You're a terrible judge of character for trusting in me, though."

It was Jiemba's turn to smile, "I don't think so. I think this is the beginning of a beautiful friendship, sis."

"You know what? I'm inclined to agree." Ewie said, before leaning her head on Jiemba's shoulders to rest.

It'd been a long day, and she was tired enough to not care about the gawking stares of their fellow passengers, or the racing of Jiemba's heartbeat pulsing under her head's weight. If today hadn't earned her a reprieve from the Holy Trinidad, she wasn't sure what could. It was time for Ewaldine "Ewie" Enders to go home.

CAELESTIS

Finley Harper

Featured in Issue #81

RAINBOWS SKITTER ACROSS THE cracked plaster wall from behind the drapes. The window rattles, and there's a *whoosh*, a *thrumming*—wings outside. But by the time Galant has bolted from bed and cast the curtain open, it's too late. The dragon is already soaring high above, glittering night slashing through the dawn. Galant can't breathe until Caelestis has gone.

Then a gleam draws her attention down two storeys to the centre of the square. A crystal ball the size of a knight's helm floats in the central fountain. It glows with ever-changing colours: forest-green, ice-blue, shell-pink. She presses her forehead and fingertips to the windowpane. If she could, she'd leap down through it.

The surrounding townhouses and shops still blur into one another in the crepuscular light, but window after window is brightening with lit oil lamps and candles. Galant hauls her woollen robe over her nightshirt and slams the door behind her as she races barefoot down the common stairs. Ms Wren shoves past, and Galant yells, "Hey," as her hip bangs into the railing.

Her protest dissolves in a burst of laughter as she and the rest of the boarding house inhabitants bunch in the foyer, held back by the heavy oak door. It's always a competition to get here first. Lightly built, yet strong from her work tending the town gardens, Ms Wren always wins. She wrenches the door open and falls out, followed moments later by her girlfriend, Ms Guante, who's softer, shapely as a Roman goddess. Then Galant, of shorter and more solid stock, squeezes out alongside tall, lanky Mr Hiriwa. As the light from the globe falls upon his features, it strips years away so his youth is visible again.

Feet slapping the cobbles—and without ripping a toenail this time—Galant is third to reach the fountain. She leans over the dimpled stone edge of the bowl, catching her breath. Ms Guante is already lifting the globe from where it's nestled beneath the central statue of a boar-man—Varras, the local forest deity. The globe casts a pink sheen across her eyes. As she tilts her face towards the rooftops, water drips unnoticed down to her elbows and down the dangling lace frills of her sleeves.

Though Ms Wren, too, must be eager for the dragon's gift, she gently folds her girlfriend's lace cuffs back so they won't be soaked, and only then eases the sphere from Ms Guante's hold into her own. Turning to the sky, her face shines as if an angel has spread luminous wings above her. She grows still as the statue of Varras. Then Mr Hiriwa peels her fingers from the crystal. As he takes it for himself, his jaw drops and he looks up, eyes glazing with tears.

All three are motionless at the edge of the fountain; unseeing, focussed on something other. Whispers and laughter bounce between the buildings as the townspeople pour into the square from all corners. News of the gift has spread, although the sun is only just dusting the roof slates.

Galant's heart quickens as she curves her hands around the shining surface of the ball. The crystal feels warm and alive like a dragon's egg might as it hatches. The noise of the gathering crowd fades as if snatched by a sudden wind. Beneath her fingers, the changing colours are like a kaleidoscope turned upon multiple worlds; each fragment birthed only moments before disappearing into the next. A pulse slices through her—and it's not her own heart.

She's knee-deep in grass, wielding a shield, gripping a sword. There's weight behind her shoulders—she can flex it if she chooses. When she does, the air thrums in four directions, and she lifts until the soles of her boots hover above the ripe sprays of seeds. Ahead, the sky is red with war.

Everywhere, there are monsters; in the sky and on the plain. Angels and demons, vampires, hunters and werebeasts snarl and tear at one another. In a dazzling flash, two collide. An accident, but Galant can tell as they circle each other and begin a dance that this will become an alliance. More—they will fall in love, though they don't yet know it. As they move, they sound like air and sea; they crackle with fire and ice. Their expressions are ferocious, but each has what the other lacks. Piece by piece they break each other's armour. Their passion shakes the air from Galant's lungs as they bleed and draw closer. She *needs* to witness—

The sun bursts over the horizon. She casts her shield arm up, protecting her eyes, and when she lowers it, blinking, morning is blazing across the roofs.

Galant grips the edge of the fountain, losing the sense of warm steel in her palm to rough, cold stone. The sound of the water tumbling is a dull echo of weapons clashing. Through the ripples, copper and silver coins glint at the bottom of the bowl. Each has been dropped by one of her neighbours—a wish for the dragon to return.

A sugary scent teases her nostrils. People are thronging around the bakery on the corner. There, Mr Hiriwa is in conversation with a young red-haired woman. He's offering her a pastry. Strolling away from them, arms linked, Ms Guante and Ms Wren are heading back to the boarding house with a bundle of baguettes.

The only one left at the fountain is Galant.

She presses her palm to her sternum. Each time, the pain is worse, not that she's telling anyone. Pastries won't ease this hunger. The warning that it could be this way for some poor soul came to her too late. And even if she'd heard before she made the town her home, it wouldn't have stopped her. She'd never known addiction. She'd never found romantic love.

Yet the love that flavours the dragon's dreams is as addictive as poppy milk. Galant can only yearn for the void each dream leaves to be filled. To this end, she's tried eating cakes with magical spices, drowning herself in wine matured in the cathedral, even tripping on the aromas from the flowers Ms Wren creates in the town gardens. All useless attempts to inspire her own dreams. She can only wait until Caelestis returns, and there's no telling when that will be. It could be tomorrow night. It could be years.

Or, she could plead with the dragon to feed her.

Her chest hitches at that thought, a half-laugh, half-sob. Dragons don't feed you. It's the other way around—or that's the common wisdom.

Ms Dresden, who runs the thrift shop, has warned her of addiction, and called to her again last time, as Galant was leaving with her arms full of bedroom drapes: *Wait, dearie! Did you know, Caelestis has a hoard? A mountain of treasure, they say. Dreams of all kinds, enough to drown in. Very rarely, some poor soul tries to steal one. Foolish! She guards them as ferociously as any dragon does their gold.*

The old woman is mischievous, knowing the effect her 'warning' will have as surely as any spell caster. Galant shivers, goosebumps rising on her arms. Can Caelestis really be that ferocious? She brings the town gifts, for Varras' sake. What does anyone know of her, truly?

What do I know?

Twice since she's made her home here, Galant has thrown the drapes back fast enough to glimpse the dragon close-up. Gunmetal-grey teeth, glittering black scales. Were those teeth really as long and razor-like as she remembers? Her eyes had been blurred with sleep. And those talons—could they really be as sharp as the farmer's scythes they resemble? They've never marked the gifts they carry.

She can't deny that the dragon is huge and doesn't need claws or talons to crush a human. But if she can find that hoard, she can plead with Caelestis face to…well, jaws. And then, if Caelestis doesn't eat her, the emptiness in her chest might be filled.

◆

A quick stop in her room for travelling clothes, her backpack and her dagger is all the delay Galant can handle. Soon, she's bounding through the town and out the stone arch in the wall. The self-appointed township guards and their followers shout malign accusations after her. She refused to join their number when she arrived; so now, this. Galant considers shouting back—she's innocent of their dreamt-up accusations—but that will only slow her down. If the town had a gate, they'd lock it shut behind her. But a gate doesn't exist, so it sucks to be them.

Outside the wall, the air is golden with sun and scented with dirt. Birds chirp all around. She brushes through the wild grasses that line the track until it leads her deeper into the forest and under a thick canopy of oak and ash, where fallen leaves muffle her tread. Dappled light makes it hard to see clearly. The path vanishes under the leaves, but she simply heads away from the town wall until it's barred from sight behind thick trunks.

As she turns in a circle, it dawns on Galant that she's lost. The canopy overhead is so lush, it hides any glimpse of the mountain. Perhaps deliberately, for in the forest, the trees shift without ceasing; mostly, too slowly for anyone to see, but an occasional traveller has witnessed them tearing their roots abruptly from the soil.

Last time she came through here, the path hadn't stayed hidden for long. She'd been looking for the town and had eventually spied its towers in the distance through the trees. But now, even her boots leave no tracks. She's been careful to scuff the moss from fallen branches and to kick leaves aside, yet when she turns, she can't see where she's just walked.

Is this your *magic, Caelestis? You don't want me to find your hoard?*

Her spine itches between her shoulder blades, and she gathers her cloak around her, clutching it at her breastbone. The creatures that live in the forest are capricious. They could have her walk in circles until she starves and then they'll feed off what's left of her body. It would be safest to turn back. She would swear on Varras's third eye that if she announces her intention loudly, the path will open up.

But...

When she closes her eyes, the sky is red. A frisson runs across her skin like lightning about to strike. She can *almost* see them, that beautiful, monstrous pair in their wild embrace. They live in other dreams as well, though their forms always change. They feel so close—and yet she can't dream them on her own. The need to witness them saving each other, and to know the intensity of their love, is a hook in her heart, as sharp and sure as one of Caelestis's talons.

Her hand falls to her dagger, a gift from her best friend she grew up with when she left her old town. The well-worn grip is a comfort. It's seen her through this forest before, spearing her food and scaring off bandits. Now, she draws it out and strikes a young branch from a rowan bush, a thin cane covered in foliage.

She glances around. There's no one here to laugh. She's no mage, but it's well known that rowan is a magical plant. Also, that in this forest, dreams influence reality (so she can't risk sleeping). However, she suspects that the closer she is to the dragon's lair, the stronger the forest's magic.

Holding the rowan branch before her, Galant closes her eyes and imagines it bursting into bloom. She whispers to the forest: "Flowers, tight clusters of white rowan flowers, densely packed white petals, pale yellow stamens..."

A breeze tugs at her cloak and her hair. The branch tugs at her fingers. Her eyes open onto long oval leaves with serrated edges. She sucks in her lip, peering through them, and her heart stutters. A spray of white behind the leaves. White flowers, covering the side facing away from her.

A smile rises through her.

♦

The magic only works on the side that faces Caelestis—or so Galant hopes. What else but the dragon's magic could call such blooms into existence? She clambers over boulders and between trunks, striking fresh branches as she needs them. The trees whisper to her, but they can no longer trick her. She continues for what feels like hours, until her legs ache and the sun's rays hold an autumn hue. Eventually she's climbing past prickly, stubby bushes up the silver-grey stone of the mountain.

As a dark crescent appears above an outcrop upslope, a gust of wind chills the sweat at her hairline. Her cloak thumps, blowing chaotically now she's left the forest. She holds tight to a knobbly trunk and turns to see how far she's come.

Below, the town is a stubborn island in a sea of forest that spreads to the horizon. A hazy gold glow gives the world a dreamlike feel. Soon dusk will fall.

Her stomach twists with hunger she can no longer ignore. She pulls a hunk of yesterday's bread from her back bag, a stalk of dried dates, and some hard cheese. But the action makes her wonder: will she arrive just as Caelestis needs to eat?

Maybe it's no accident that the thing lodged in her heart feels like a hook. She's a hapless fish on a line.

Her best friend would counsel her to eat and find somewhere to sleep wedged in by bushes, and in the morning, go home safe.

As she snatches her meal and watches the horizon, red spreads through the gold like blood into a tumbler of whisky. Birds rise in a clamour of screeches. They're a storm of silhouettes across the sunset. All at once, Galant exists in two places. The cold stone under her palms is cold steel; her grip on her sword tightens at the monsters' arrival.

In both worlds, in her mind's eye, she can see Caelestis. The dragon is crouched at the mouth of the cavern above, talons latched around the outcrop, golden eyes absorbing the dreamscape.

She must have crouched there hundreds of times. No—she's immortal, so it could be thousands or more, before she wrought her vision into the gift she just gave the town. No wonder her dreams are vivid.

And how much more has Caelestis seen? When she flies, she soars above everything. She can cover the world. Has she turned everything she's seen into dreams?

No wonder Galant must climb on.

◆

Inside the entrance to the cavern, sunset washes the walls crimson. The rocky ceiling arches high, then disappears into a dark throat. A mottled tongue of large, smooth pebbles winds down the centre. Galant can imagine Caelestis's serpentine tail sweeping bigger rocks to either side. Shattering where they landed, they've formed misshapen rows of jagged teeth.

Galant treads as silently as she can along the right side of the cave. Occasionally, a rock shifts beneath her, and clacks onto another. The small explosion makes her heart hammer.

As the wall turns, damp and gritty beneath her outstretched fingers, the light fades. *Dammit, I haven't packed a lantern.* Although, that might have warned Caelestis of her approach. Galant stops and closes her eyes, stretching her hearing, even her sense of smell.

She can hear her own pulse, the blood rushing through her ears.

The wind sighs as it brushes her cheeks.

Is that cinnamon? The scent of dreams? Her stomach flutters. She feels ahead along the rock, and something clinks under her boot. She catches a cry in her throat and breathes out slowly. Casting out with her toe, there's more—the surface shifts. She crouches, reaching forwards, and her fingertips brush metal.

Cold, smooth edges. Thin, flat pieces.

Coins.

♦

The coins lead upslope. Falling onto her knees, Galant can feel no limit to them. As she crawls on, they clink like chains sliding over one another and her knees sink into them. Her eyes are adjusting—faint gleams appear, more as she looks up, until she's sliding and clinking along the ruffled surface of a moonlit river. A mountain of coins, more than she imagined existed. Millions, trillions. Yet Caelestis has never demanded tribute, or anything in exchange for her gifts. She couldn't have carried them all here, so did she make them somehow? Are they fragments of her dreams? Each one of them part of her magic?

It's the only explanation.

How large is her mind to have held all this?

Galant swallows. *Why am I doing this again?*

An arm's length away, orbs the size of oranges glow among the coins. She can't look too closely or they'll draw her in. They shimmer with pink and sea-green—colours that remind her of wet sand and seaweed necklaces—and sea snails crawling over the edges of the chipped blue bowl that she's holding, full of shells she's just collected. She squeals: those shells were meant to be empty—

No—!

"Too real," she pants, needing the sound of her own voice to confirm she's back. She's not a child, and she hasn't actually squealed. Her whisper is real; so is the heavy sound of her breath and the crunch of coins under her knees.

Even the small dreams are powerful.

♦

It's more like climbing a series of rapids than a river. Past a huge, natural rock pillar that rises through the coins, the bigger and brighter dreams clustered at the top make it easier to see, yet above them is an impossible, unnatural blackness. As Galant stares into it, a trickle of sweat tickles her throat. There's a sound like heavy rain approaching. Pinpoints of light coalesce into the shape of the dragon's forelimb, sweeping across the surface of the coins. Gathering her treasures to her chest, Caelestis becomes distinct from the pile of metal and rock.

She's a dark angel, wings like voids spread over her hoard. The talons at their joints shine like lovingly polished daggers. Her neck twists sinuously, bringing her massive head around, golden eyes narrowing on Galant. Caelestis lowers her snout, sliding it forward over her dreams.

Galant trembles like a stalk of grass. The dragon has more teeth than she remembers seeing through her bedroom window; a forest of curved needles. When Caelestis's jaw lowers, Galant can see past those needle teeth into the red glow of her gullet. Her breath is a desert wind burning Galant's hair, dowsing her in cinnamon. Her mind flails—

She's in a dark chamber, staring into smoke that drifts from the spout of a brass lamp. As she reaches for the handle, which is shaped like a cobra, it's watching her... *No.* Her watcher is distant. He's past the lamp, crouching by an enormous column. A young man with wolfish features and unsettling amber eyes. She's seen him before, yet he doesn't know her, and he's glaring... *Not at me.* At whatever she can feel close to her back. A whisper from there sinks into her ear; the barest brush of a finger spreads frost through her jaw. The place where her neck and shoulder meet throbs.

But mist feathers past, obscuring her vision until the veiled glow of Caelestis's eye appears.

"COME HERE. LET ME SEEE YOUUU..."

Her voice is the deep sound of a boiling spring reverberating through a tunnel. It vibrates through her hoard, compelling Galant to obey. The coins slide, then they're pulling her down as she tries to climb up, closing over her hands and calves, giving way like quicksand.

Caelestis tosses her head, nostrils flaring. Her hiss resounds through the cavern. Vibrating coins engulf Galant's thighs.

"I'm going to drown!" Galant yells. This isn't even how she'd imagined she'd die. She should never have come here; never given in to greed.

A sound like thousands of chains rattles behind her, then something collides with her back and launches her up in a torrent of gold. Her spine arches helplessly as she flies towards Caelestis's teeth. A claw flashes past, then she's jerked to a stomach-lurching halt, caught by the back of her tunic. She strains to inhale, a horrible strangled sound.

But swinging past below are the most precious dreams—baubles that hold entire worlds. Baubles no one but Caelestis has ever seen. And now Galant. Though her heart is pounding with the shock of near-death, she can't help but reach for them. Endless twists and turns in their depths draw her in. Some are the warm, abyssal red of embers. Others are the profound blue said to be found in the hearts of icebergs.

"WHAT DO YOU DREEEAMMM?"

The power of Caelestis's voice drags Galant back. The dragon has set her down on her side, caging her with those scythe-like talons. Their reflective surfaces are a safer place to look than the baubles behind them. This close, Galant should fear Caelestis, and she surely does, except... Rolling onto her elbows, she lifts her chin. "You haven't eaten me. Or even scratched me."

In fact, Caelestis has saved her from drowning in gold. This is enough reassurance that Galant can give her answer, though the dragon may not like what she hears. "I have no dreams." Well. That's not strictly true. "I mean, none that I remember." Risking a higher look, she meets the dragon's long. golden eye with its monstrous, vertical pupil.

"WHY ARE YOU HERE?"

"I wanted to see you."

Silence. Galant senses her answer is inadequate.

"And...I wanted more of your dreams. I wanted to ask you if I could see, could share—"

"I AM NOT READY TO SHARE."

"Forgive me." She bows her head. Her impatience is unforgivable. She should have waited years if she had to, knowing that Caelestis would one day fly over the town.

"BUT...SINCE YOU ARE HERE." Caelestis lifts a talon and nudges a globe toward Galant with a soft chink. A wag of a claw tip invites her to look. "THERE WILL BE A PRICE."

Galant exhales slowly. A price. Isn't there always?

She glances down at herself, at her arms. Her sleeves are dirty from clambering over rocks and coins, torn in many places from her trek through the forest. Her bruised skin shows through the gaps. Spreading her fingers displays her ripped and bloody nails. Will Caelestis want a ruined hand?

Her legs are in better shape, protected by her woollen trousers and knee-high, scuffed boots. Will Caelestis want a foot?

She gulps.

"A DREAM," the dragon adds. Is that a smirk in her tone?

"I told you," Galant says. "I don't have any of my own."

In the long silence that follows, she can hear Caelestis's heart, the massive beat pulling her own into alignment.

"I DON'T BELIEVE YOU."

♦

Caelestis cradles Galant tenderly in her claws. Ten thousand teeth glitter along the dragon's wicked smile. Her nostrils flare and a gust of sweet cinnamon sends sparks flying through Galant's mind.

They give way to a river flowing through a forest between two towns; she's sailed here before, only now she remembers. As she explores anew, Caelestis flies alongside her. The dragon's tail whips through the trees, shaking them like a tempest, yet never breaking a twig. Her presence is constant. Together, they witness storms and battles, Galant's nightmares and daydreams, fears and victories. Galant is the constantly shapeshifting hero of her journey, yet the dragon's heroes join her, the monsters she adores, fighting at her side. Her heart soars when the two declare their love for one another and finally embrace.

After hours, days, years, her eyes crack open. She's curled around a familiar, shimmering surface. If she touches it just the right way, it will expand around her consciousness. The tip of a talon, sharp as the tool of an engraver, slides over it near her face. Colours swirl in the wake of Caelestis's claw, yet it leaves no trace when it lifts away.

"IT IS READY."

♦

None of Galant's dreams have prepared her for the sight of the town directly below, so small that it looks like a toy. From the sky, she has to wonder how anything but dreams could really matter down there. The guards' taunts as she left feel less substantial now than a grain of sand. Seen from above, the town wall hints at bigger conflicts in the past, and the many-shaped houses and towers speak of occupants from every corner of the world. The flowering gardens and pools decorating the streets are every bit as beautiful as the dragon's hoard. She can see why Caelestis keeps returning.

The dragon's wings sound like crashing waves as she pulls closer to the sun. Every beat blasts cold air down Galant's face and body. She should be afraid, but her blood hums too vibrantly. They spiral up and up into the light—and then Caelestis dives.

Galant's stomach floats. Her cloak tugs at her neck, her hair tears at her scalp. Caelestis roars and the world shakes. Her voice rocks through Galant to her fingertips around the orb—she yells with Caelestis, as alive as the flames in the dragon's belly.

The square expands until she can see the individual bricks in the townhouses. She plummets past her own bedroom window. Caelestis releases her, and she and the dream she's clutching land with a giant splash. Surfacing, gasping for breath beneath the statue of Varras, she flicks her wet hair back, every burnt strand.

To one side of the fountain, Ms Wren and Ms Guante are gaping at her. But above, Caelestis circles higher into the sky, scales sparkling like stars. Her yellow eyes gleam. "RETURN SOON, FRIEND!"

I will. Galant waves as she climbs to her feet, shedding water like she's just shed all her expectations of dragons. A wind gusts down, fragrant with the scent that in her fear she first mistook for cinnamon. It's more than that: it's ambrosia, and it rings with a sound more divine than any she's heard in the cathedral, despite the monstrous timbre of Caelestis's voice. Galant's chest is so full that her eyes overflow. Who knew a dragon could laugh?

That night, she dreams. She's with her best friend, and they're flying with Caelestis.

DINGO & SISTER

Nikky Lee

Featured in Issue #78

T HE RED DUST IS so fine it seeps through my scarf, caking in my mouth. With each breath, it tickles the back of my throat. Belly down in the dirt, the afternoon sun stings the back of my legs as I watch the men below.

Patience, sister. Dingo lies alert beside me, her fur almost the same colour as the earth, ears pricked as she listens. *Our time will come.*

Thirst pools saliva under my tongue and I swallow, tasting earth, catching the cough in my throat before I scare our game away. It's a small camp, tents pitched among the saltbush in the shade of one lone mulga tree.

Smoke from the camp wafts up to us, bringing scents of wild mutton and sandalwood: thick, creamy and rich. Dingo rests her head on her paws, patient as always, but her nose twitches, scenting.

Sheena once said sandalwood was the most expensive wood in the old-world—back when this land was whole, before the seas swallowed the coast and birthed a sea from Melbourne to Adelaide. But now, here in the outback, if it burns it goes on the fire. I breathe in the cloud, savouring it, hoping it might fool my empty stomach. It doesn't.

The sun sinks lower. Still, we don't move. Just as the last dregs of red seep below the horizon, Dingo shifts, raises her head, yawns. Dusk is our time. The witching hour, folks of the old-world called it. Dingo calls it the hunting hour.

I rise, shedding dust, muscles quivering from lying still so long.

Time to eat.

The men don't hear us come.

Together, Dingo and I steal into their camp. Dingo runs low, belly skimming the ground, ears alert, eyes crescent slivers of firelight beside me. I skip across the still-warm earth, rock to weed to rock again—anywhere that won't leave prints. My shoes, soft leather worn in from all our walking, make no sound.

We take their water first. I slip the plastic water bottles from their packs, tucking them under one arm. Dingo sniffs out their supplies: tinned fruit, wrapped crackers. A meagre fare. But I take them anyway.

A shout from the fire freezes us.

"You fucking *pig*; you drank it all?" The voice is male, angry, directed over the flames. Something thuds to the ground: an empty flask, tethered lid off and clacking against the metal.

My heart hits the roof of my mouth, but I stay the urge to flee.

Humans are hunters. They see movement better than all else. Dingo's lessons sound in my head. I sink to the ground instead, gaze never leaving the group by the fire. A bearded man stands with his knuckles bunched over a cowering boy.

Two others, a man and woman, sit at the fireside and stare at the flames.

"Are you trying to kill us?" the man growls. "Our supplies have to last until Alice. We're not even halfway there!"

"I know, but—" The boy licks his cracked lips.

Warmth presses against my side. Soft. Dingo. She tenses as the bearded man thrusts a yellowed finger into the boy's face.

"We're all thirsty, boy. *Everyone*." His finger swings out to the glint of metal in the distance. Rail tracks. The same tracks I've been prowling for months. The rail sleepers are cracked and splintered, dried out in the desert sun.

"Don't like it and you can follow them back to hell," the man warns.

The boy's eyes search for an escape. They flit across the camp, taking in the saltbushes, the grass and rock. And me.

We stare at each other for what feels like an age. He lets out a croak. Points.

They turn, see me, blink oafishly in the night. And then their voices explode from beside the fire.

"What the f—" the brute says.

"Don't scare her—" This from the boy.

The woman springs up, rage spasming her features. "The water, Harley, she's got our water!"

Heat surges down my limbs. Dingo's lips peel back, exposing teeth. She springs from my shadow, jaws snapping.

Run sister!

I don't look back.

◆

I feel the brush of Dingo's return. It's late, the night deep and cold as she nuzzles in beside me, muzzle wet. I press my fingers into her fur: more wet. It coats my hands. I rise from my bed under the saltbush, its bristle leaves catching at my scarf. Alarm thumps in my throat, along with a strange unfolding of my stomach.

You're hurt?

Dingo licks her nose, then mine. *I am fine, sister. A scratch, nothing more.*

My belly knots and unknots. I've felt this before and I clutch my elbows, hugging them tight. Dingo worms her head underneath one arm. *I am still with you*, she says. *Go back to sleep.*

We settle. I wrap my arms around Dingo's neck, bury my face in her fur and breathe in her scent: smoke and sandalwood. *Promise you won't leave?*

I promise.

◆

They find us at dawn.

Hands grab my ankles and drag me from the shelter of the saltbush. I scream and kick, snarl and spit like a feral cat, knocking away more hands as they try to hold me still. My teeth close around someone's forearm and I bite *hard*, tasting blood. But my teeth aren't sharp like Dingo's. Mine are blunt, and instead of a scream I get a grunt in response.

"Fucking bitch."

And then they sit on me. They throw me belly-down onto the red soil and pin me there, arses on my back, boots clouding my vision.

"Hell," someone huffs. "She's mental."

"Well she would be to rob us, wouldn't she?" another chimes. I recognise the voice—the angry man from the camp. The sound, his sound, rumbles above me and my breath catches. I knew another voice like that once. A shadow looms out of my memory, fists thudding into Sheena, who's wrapped her arms around me.

No, don't think about it. *Dingo, where are you?*

I'm coming, Sister. Hold tight.

"Look at her." The big man again. Someone kicks my scuffed and worn boots. "Skinny as shit. The dirt she's lying on is worth more."

A hand tugs my matted braids. "You can't fuck dirt, isn't that right little rat?" This from the woman.

I try to muster a response, a growl—anything. But my voice is dead in my throat. My chest hurts, crushed under their weight.

Why did you leave me, Dingo? You promised you wouldn't!

I writhe under them like a desert snake. What a thing it would be to turn on them, muscles warm and quick in the morning sun. I'd sink my fangs into their calves, pump venom into their veins.

But some people already have venom there.

A cuff to the ear sends my head spinning.

"Look at her. She's all bone." The big man again, disgust ripe in his voice. "No house will take her."

"If she's not worth anything, why not let her go?" This voice is softer, nervous, and I know it's the boy. If not for him, they'd never have seen me last night. They'd never have followed me back here.

The woman snorts. "The camps will take anyone with two legs, a hand and breath left in their lungs. All they gotta do is dig."

I am here.

Face half-mashed into the dirt, I peer past the boots of my captors. A red shadow slinks across the earth, burnt orange eyes bright in the morning. Dingo. A half sob rises in my throat. Dingo is here. She's not abandoned me yet.

My captors think my sniffing is about them.

"Cry all you like, desert rat; you shouldn't have robbed us." The woman leers into my vision, hair drooping over her sunburnt face in tight braids—like mine, but blonde. She's from the south, too. Where it's too dry to wash hair often, so most women braid it. Perhaps she also left the coast behind to travel inland in the hopes of a better life.

A hackled sneer twitches her lips.

Or maybe not.

Her hand snakes out, grabs my hair, nails digging in between the plaits, and her face comes very close to mine. She smells of smoke and iron. "What did you do with our water?" Her eyes dart over my body, searching, and seeing nothing, adds, "Hidden it, eh? Little cunt."

And then I see it through the arm of her sweat-stained shirt. A revolver—antique even by old-world standards—hugs her ribs in a holster under the cotton.

I am ready, sister, Dingo says, and I sense her behind me, crouched and quivering, ready to—

No!

Dingo goes still, body turning ridged as stone.

No! I tell her again. *I can't lose you.*

The woman smacks my head into the ground so hard I see stars. Her palm presses at my temples as she grinds her weight into me, pushing my cheek into the dirt.

"Silence won't protect you, rat," she says. Then the pressure is gone. "Get her up," she snaps. "Search the area; she won't have hidden it far away."

And all at once I understand. The big man's not in charge. She is.

◆

"In Alice, you can wash in a whole tub of water," Sheena says as we squat over our bucket of rationed water, dipping facecloths into it and rubbing the sweat and oil from our skin. "One day, we'll get out of this sandpit." She stares out the dust-crusted glass of our living room window. "We'll go together."

It's a scandalous idea, to have that much water. But the people in Alice fared better than those on the coast. Where we had encroaching sea and salt pans, they had basins of underground water. My gaze slides to the shadow on the couch and the empty bottles nestled in the crook of his elbow—water might be short, but spirits were always easy to come by. Ships brought it across the Inland Sea from Melbourne by the crateful. People bought it in droves—desperate for a drink, even though consuming it only made their thirst worse.

"Just us?" I whisper.

Sheena dabs at my face with a cloth, careful to skirt the bruises. "Of course. Once we've saved enough, we'll buy passage on one of the caravans. You and me. A fresh start."

I reach for my sister's hand, my fingers slim and small in hers, and squeeze. "I'd like that."

The pop of a log on a fire snaps me awake; a string of embers rises into a moonless sky and the pinpricks of ten thousand stars.

My heart bucks, kicking my ribs. *Dingo.*

I am here. It is not looking good, sister.

My senses shift, unfurl, and I feel her there in the darkness behind me. A familiar, comforting weight on the edge of my thoughts—fierce and tender all at once. I release my breath and rest my head against the mulga tree they've tied me to. Its small, spindly limbs are rough and twisted against my back. The spiked leaves poke through my scarf and shirt. The night is cool, but under me the earth is still warm. Sunset was not long ago then.

Figures move about the camp. The woman—the leader—sits next to the fire, poking the wood around a billy pot. Yellow light washes her features, turning the lines in her face dark and hard. Behind, the big man rummages in a pack, swearing as he goes. A movement—a shuffle closer to the flames—and I spot the boy huddled so close to the fire it's a wonder he's not set his threadbare jeans alight. It's not cold that makes him huddle like that—though it will soon. Right now his eyes follow the big man as he stomps about the camp, cursing about his lack of smokes.

"If you've taken them—" he threatens the woman, who's not having a bar of it.

"Fuck off, Harley. I didn't take your damn cigarettes."

I flex my hands behind the mulga, testing the strength of the rope around my wrists again. It's been hours. My shoulders burn and my butt aches from sitting.

Rope is no match for my teeth. Dingo shivers forward in the dark, and there's a soft snuff from behind the mulga's leaves. A wet tongue licks my palm. I shift my weight from one side to the other, trying to bring the feeling back into my legs. I want to be ready so I can run.

"Stop fidgeting, Rat." I jump, look up to find the woman staring at me over the fire, eyes narrowed.

Get back!

Dingo shrinks away. The woman shows no sign of seeing her.

"Let her be, Rosa." The words issue out of the night, and another figure looms into the firelight carrying a dead rabbit. He's tall and older than the rest by at least a dozen years, with leather for skin. Thin too—almost to the point of withered, like a desert weed.

"You can fuck off too, Arlen. I'll call her what I like."

The newcomer ignores her.

Something about him makes my stomach clench as he drops the scrawny rabbit to the earth and begins to gut and skin it. He does it with deft strokes. His hunting knife cuts open the belly and slides under the fur as if it were silk. The entrails go on the fire with a hiss.

This man, not Rosa, or Harley or the boy, is the one who tracked me. I'm sure of it. This man is dangerous. He knows how to survive the desert.

Dingo shies further into the shadows of the mulga. *I do not like it, sister.*

Wait until they sleep, I bide. *Then we run.*

Apart from his warning to Rosa, Arlen ignores me. The rabbit goes on the fire and when it is done, the four of them crowd around it like crows over a carcass, fingers pecking the bones clean. They are an odd group, I think. The size of their packs suggests they're a caravan—or trying to be. But they're not. Not really. There's too much discord compared to the other caravans I've preyed upon. Too much suspicion. Too much distrust.

Perhaps that was why they caught me. Their guards were already up.

But there is one thing they share with those who have come before. They're running. Running away from the hell that is the coast, or perhaps from something else. Either way, they're trying to cross the desert—just like all the others.

Whereas I can't bring myself to leave.

"They're not always like this." I start as a voice sounds beside me. The boy. I'd been so consumed with Tracker Arlen to notice him leave the fireside and cross the camp to me. "I mean, Harley's a prick, but he listens to Rosa. Here." He holds up a handful of rabbit meat—mostly gristle, "you must be hungry."

I jerk my hands behind the mulga, shifting so he can see my wiggling fingers trapped in the rope binding. He gets my meaning and sighs, shaking his head.

"Rosa said I can't untie you."

Worth a try.

He picks up a piece of meat and puts it to my mouth. I don't hesitate. I chomp down, levering it between my teeth before crunching through the cartilage and swallowing. The same goes for the next, and the next.

"I'm Mason," he says when I take the last bit. He waits for me to respond and the silence lengthens.

"What's...your name?" he prompts at last.

I stare back at him, blank-faced, saying nothing. He sighs again and holds up a canteen. One of the ones I'd stolen. "You thirsty?"

A stupid question. He uncaps the lid and lets me take a sip. I get just enough to wet my mouth before the bottle is ripped away.

"Stop wasting our fucking water," Harley growls through a plume of smoke. He's found his cigarettes. He holds Mason's canteen in one hand, fingers gripped around the neck.

"She has to eat too," Mason says, but mostly to his feet.

Harley is so quick I barely see it. The butt of his cigarette blurs as his hand moves, connecting with Mason's cheek in a fleshy clap of skin-on-skin. Mason's head wobbles, knees sag.

"She's drunk her fill already, idiot. Just leave the goods alone." He stalks off, Mason's water bottle still clutched in his hand. A minute later, he takes a sip.

I wait for them to sleep. Once they do, I will call Dingo back to set her teeth to my ropes. But they don't sleep. Not all at once. The three adults take the night in shifts.

This may take longer than I thought, I tell Dingo.

She circles the camp again. *I don't like it.*

I close my eyes and rest my head on the mulga. *Patience, sister.*

◆

We follow the rail tracks. Day in, day out. Heat beats down on us and the dust, washing the horizon in a haze. Every morning, they take up the rope to my bound hands and lead me along, lest their cash cow get away before reaching Alice. I follow like an obedient dog. Every night they find something to tie me to. And when there's no suitable tree or rock, they tie me to the tracks themselves. On those nights, I don't sleep. Instead I lie there, aching, and hope they're right about the trains not running. Not enough fuel—or at least, not enough of the affordable kind—that's what Rosa said when Mason questioned it.

As they take turns at watch, so do Dingo and I. We wait, ready to seize the moment when one of them succumbs. It will happen soon. They are pushing hard, walking from daybreak to dusk. Desperate to make the crossing.

On the third day, we reach a ghost town. Marla, according to Arlen. It's nothing more than an abandoned roadhouse and a few cottages. The town's water tower is dry and Rosa curses, instructing the others to ration their water: two mouthfuls a day. One in the morning; one at night. I get one.

On the fourth day it comes, though not in the way I expect. It's noon, the sun high overhead. Dust sticks to our sweat so there's no telling Rosa's pale skin from Mason's tan—everyone is simply red. One moment Harley is walking beside the tracks, following them as usual. The next, the earth gives under his foot—an old rabbit burrow—and the sand crumples away as his boot sinks in.

There's a pop and a snap, and Harley goes down with a howl, clutching his shin.

When he finally lets Arlen remove his boot, his ankle is twisted and swelling like an overripe tomato. Arlen pulls Rosa to one side.

"It's bad," he mutters to her once they're out of earshot of everyone—everyone but Dingo and me.

"Shit." Rosa rubs her face, leaving red and white smears down her cheeks.

"He won't be able to walk," Arlen says. "Not like we need him to. We're three days out from Kulgera and it's another five days from there to Alice." He puts a hand on her shoulder, leans in closer. "Have you kept it clean? Made sure there's no sand in it?"

Rosa's hand goes to the holster at her side. She chews her lip; nods. Mason's hold on my rope quivers as he tries to comfort Harley, stopping only when the burly man catches the collar of his shirt and shoves him away. The movement jars Harley's leg and he grimaces, eyes glistening as he draws in one breath through his teeth, then another.

He catches sight of Rosa and Arlen's faces as they return, and underneath the dust his cheeks drain of colour. Rosa pulls her revolver from under her shirt, flicks off the safety.

"Wait," Harley says. "You can't—"

"Rosa..." Mason begins, horror dawning. "You don't mean to—"

She rounds on the boy. "Will you carry him all the way to Alice?" she snarls, her dirt-slicked skin turning her face into that of a monster crawled up from the earth's underbelly. Then she looks away, and the mask cracks. "It is kinder this way."

"But we can rig up a stretcher, pull him along or—"

Arlen presses a hand to Mason's shoulder and looks him in the eye. "It's not just Harley; it's us we have to think about too. If we slow down, we'll run out of water."

"But—" Mason protests, and when he can't think of anything more to say, he closes his mouth and stares at the dirt. I watch the whole exchange, curious. Strange how he's so ready to come to the aid of a man who'd leave him for dead without a thought, were the roles reversed. I'd have thought he'd be happy.

I had been.

Holding hands on the street, Sheena and I had let that shadow burn inside his house—his booze adding to the fire's heat—and I had been glad. Glad he was gone.

"He was already dead," Sheena said, a little defensively. She didn't need to explain what she'd done—not to me—but she did anyway. "He died the day Ma did."

Then together, with nowhere else left to go, we started walking. And I hadn't cared about the thing we'd left behind.

But Mason is a better person than me. He cares. Like Sheena did. And he cries—as Sheena did—when he turns his back and lets Arlen guide us down the train tracks. Away from Rosa and Harley.

"We promised!" Harley cries at Rosa as we leave. His voice breaks. "You promised! No records in Alice, you said. A new start."

One hundred metres down the tracks, the revolver snaps the silence, sound ringing into the sky like a whip crack.

Rosa re-joins us.

Above, a lone wedge-tail circles. Behind, Dingo closes in on the corpse.

Nothing is ever wasted in the desert.

♦

We are getting too close, I tell Dingo. My skin bristles. Too close to *it*.

Kulgera is on the horizon. The tumbledown station lies in ruins next to the tracks—an old tourist stop for the trains. Back then, when they still ran twice a week, it had a roadhouse and a police station and a population of fifty.

Post warming population: zero. Sheena had researched thoroughly before we'd left. She'd known every stop and watering hole we'd make, every step—except for her last.

No. The hairs prickle on my neck, heart thumps in my chest. I jerk my thoughts away and shut my eyes, swallowing the hot burn in the back of my throat. Don't think—don't see her lying there…

Dingo's presence wraps around my thoughts, soft and warm. *I am here for you, sister*, she says. *Call and I'll come and tear your ropes free.*

Rosa's gun flashes through my mind's eye. The thought of that turning on Dingo—on her beautiful form still in the dirt, a red dribble of blood from her neck—smacks my heart into my ribs. Anything but that. *Not yet.* I swallow and steady my breathing. *Just stay with me.*

I will. Dingo says, and she pulls at my senses, turning my gaze back along the tracks. There, in the distance—almost lost in the haze—a four-legged shape lopes along the tracks. *I am here. I am ready.*

We enter the town. Rusted corrugated tin is about all that remains. Mason's gaze lingers on the sheets lying in the dirt. Probably thinks that he could have used one for a makeshift stretcher for Harley. Too late now. Besides, there are things hiding under those sheets and not all of them are friendly. He doesn't know it—not yet—but I do. Best line of defence: stay away.

The water tower is the same as I remember it. Windmill and well, the pump hand-driven and half-rusted. Rosa pumps it for a full minute before anything comes out, and when it does, the water is the same colour as the dirt. Red, like blood. But a few pumps later it runs clean—or clean enough.

"We'll spend the night here," Rosa says. "Drink what you can, and drink again. Don't stop until you're pissing clear."

We obey. Arlen lights a fire and we crowd around it, boiling tin beans in their can. Mason's forgotten to tie my lead rope, but I don't run. Rosa is still watching. She puffs on one of Harley's cigarettes, eyes darting from Mason, to Arlen, to me, then to the dark desert beyond—as if even the sand might judge her.

Soon. I see it in the droop of their shoulders and the way they stagger off into the night to pee. As we turn in, Mason insists he is included in the watch. Arlen and Rosa exchange a look. Arlen shrugs and turns for his swag.

"Fine," Rosa says.

Tonight is my chance. Tonight, I will be free.

♦

He drops off like clockwork. At first Mason fights it. His head nods hard once, twice… He jerks it up each time, blinking into the fire, before at last it lolls on his chest and stays. His hand grows lax on my rope.

Come now, I call.

Dingo hurries out of the dark, a red shape against the black, her paws a whisper in the sand. Her teeth set upon my rope—biting and tearing, but careful not to nip my skin. My eyes never leave Rosa. She snores on the other side of the fire, the shape of her revolver clear underneath her shirt.

A soft ping of thread at my wrists, and I'm free. I fling my arms around Dingo's neck and bury my face into her fur. Smoke and sandalwood. Safe and warm. Home.

Thank you, sister. Thank you.

Are you ready? Dingo says. *We must run.*

I wipe my eyes and stand. My legs are cold and stiff, but I force through the first few steps, picking my way around the fire, collecting what I need to go the rest of the way and bundling them into my scarf. I move slow, every pace considered—checking and rechecking my shadow won't fall across the others as they sleep. I give Arlen a wide berth—no sense risking it—then glance back at Rosa, smirk and step—

A hand grabs my arm. I catch the yelp in my chest, muffling it into a gasp—and spin. Mason. The firelight plays shadows across his skin, turning the whites of his eyes bright. His fingers quiver on my arm.

"Where are you going?" he hisses.

I jerk my arm free and stride on, feet quiet on the earth. Mason thumps after me, but doesn't grab again.

"Back out there?" he asks. "Alone?"

Dingo materialises out of the dark beside me. Mason stops still, stares—quivering like prey, tension running up his legs and across his shoulders. Fight or flight. His fear curls through the air, into my nose. I put a hand on Dingo's head, ruffle her ears. Mason breaths out again.

Let's go. Together we turn.

"Wait." Mason darts back to the fire. Grabs his pack. I wince as it scuffs on the earth as he drags it onto his shoulders. But Rosa and Arlen don't move. "I'm coming with you."

I stare at him for a long moment, dumbfounded—not sure I heard right. Him? With us? It has always been Dingo and me. Just us—and the desert.

Dingo pads forward, and Mason stiffens, holding his breath as she snuffs him. Her ears perk up.

Bring him.

But—

The fire pops and a pistol of flames shoots skyward. Rosa starts awake with a yelp, her hands grappling for the gun under her shirt. She finds it, relaxes, and sinks back to her swag. Then her sleep-sodden eyes rove the camp and land on the scraps of rope I've left at the fireside. She frowns at Mason's empty swag, then looks up and out into the night.

"Arlen!" she lurches to her feet, staggers over to him and shakes his shoulder. "Arlen, that little shit's let her loose. She's getting away! Get up!"

Dingo curls her mind around mine, her strength surges into my muscles, hot and brimming. The aches fall away. *Run,* she whispers. *Run.*

Together, the three of us turn and flee.

♦

The sky is growing pink when we collapse into the dirt, shuddering and shaking. The rail tracks stretch into the distance before us. Behind, the remains of Kulgera are a smudge on the horizon. Mason rolls onto his back—gasping—and claws at a stitch in his side.

"Think we lost them?"

I shake my head and try to stand. Rosa is coming. I know it as sure as I know the sun will rise tomorrow. My knees wobble and I sag back to the earth.

"Steady on," Mason says. He reaches for my hand and I jerk my arm away. He starts and blinks, a frown creasing his smooth features. "Just trying to help."

I glower at him.

Dingo nuzzles under my arm, lending me the strength of her shoulder. *He is right. You must rest, even just for a little while.*

I sigh and sink into the sand. *Fine. If you say so.*

But something inside me itches. My skin crawls. I imagine Rosa in dogged pursuit—cheeks blotched red in sunburn and anger, spittle flying as she catches me in her grip, fingers like irons around my wrists. I shiver and pull the water bottle I pilfered from the camp before I ran, and take a sip. The water clears my head. I sip again.

Mason does the same with his own bottle. Small sips—no more than a mouthful at a time. Neither of us knows when our next water stop will be. Not now. Not with Kulgera behind us. An image of a body—quiet in the morning, chest still and silent—flashes through my head. I choke and cough precious liquid up over the dirt.

It's close. Too close. I want to turn and run back along the tracks, away from that memory in the sand. But Rosa lies in that direction. I force my mouthful of water down. No choice but forward.

Mason's gaze is fixed on Dingo, wary. "You know they kill people, right?" he says.

Dingo turns on him, fur the colour of rust in the sunrise. Her hackles twitch. *So does the sun, the snake, and the spider. Do you hold them guilty too?*

I push my fingers through Dingo's fur, feeling the dust stick to my skin, staining my hands red. Dingo would never hurt me. I know this truth to the bone. When Dingo does not move, Mason shrugs, sips again from his bottle and the spell is broken. Dingo twitches then licks my cheek.

Rest. I will warn you if she comes.

I look into her eyes. It is like looking into twin suns. Sheena told me about stars once, and how they burn different colours depending on their age. Bright yellow when they're young, red when they're old. Here in the sunrise, Dingo's eyes glint ancient mahogany. The body flashes through my thoughts again, my fists clench into her fur.

Promise you won't leave?

I promise.

◆

"Rosa wasn't always like that," Mason says as we walk, following the tracks the next day. "When I was younger, she was nicer. Tried to take care of us all in the compound. But one by one, everyone left. Some struck out for the Inland Sea, hoping to buy passage to Bendigo, maybe go on to Canberra. But it's just as bad there, they say. Too many people and not enough water. And the sea just keeps coming."

I half listen, my belly balled tight like a fist. *Close. Too close.* But even I can't stay in the desert forever. I have water. And more food than I've had in months. This is my chance. A chance to reach Alice—one last push.

"In the end it was just Mum, Rosa, Harley and me. And then the fire happened. Lightning strike in the last heat wave, you know?" Mason is saying. His boots scuff the splintered sleepers. I wish he would pick up his feet properly. We're leaving quite the easy trail to follow. But then again, we're following the tracks, just like all the other pilgrims before us. Where else would we go?

"Mum sold everything that was left. Half herself as well. One lung, one kidney. Just enough to pay Rosa to take me with her and Harley."

I'm not sure why he needs to tell me this, but I let him finish.

"They used the money to hire Arlen to guide us across." Mason's fists clenched. "Then blew the rest of it on cigarettes and booze."

His story is different to mine, but also the same. Both of us are chasing a dream deep into the desert. Come to think of it, when did anyone last hear from Alice? Perhaps the city has dried up like all the rest? My heart quickens. Surely Sheena had thought to check. Surely.

A prick of cool nudges my hand: Dingo's nose. She's sensed my unease and utters a faint whine, almost too high pitched for me to hear.

We're a bunch of fucking idiots, I tell her. *We're going to die out here.*

Nonetheless, we walk on, she says.

Ahead, Mason stops, cups a hand to his brow and squints. "What's that?" He points at something round and smooth and cream-coloured lying in the dirt by the tracks. Dread settles in my stomach like a stone. He hurries over to it, brushes off the sand and shrinks back with a yelp.

A human skull rolls away from his fingers, bone dry as kindling.

We're here.

I clear my throat. Precious waste of spit and water, but I need to say it. Need to warn him. Let him prepare himself.

"It's the start of the Graveyard."

◆

"This last stretch is like the last climb on Everest," Sheena said once, months ago in the very place I stand now. She'd shown me pictures of it once—in a tattered, old-world magazine, and we'd daydreamed about being adventurers on the other side of the world. "I know you're tired and hungry, and all that water from Kulgera is heavy, but no matter what, don't stop."

Stop and you may never get up again. Her words still haunt me.

I survey the dunes. They rise red out of the land like waves, burying and uncovering the tracks with each one of their strange tides. Today, a stifling northerly breeze pushes them to meet us. The heat of it scorches my cheeks. Sweat clings to my legs, my back, my neck. How can a city survive in this country? A country so far from anywhere with these dunes—these mountains—between them and the dregs of civilisation?

Nerves stab my gut, so hard I almost double over and grunt. *What if Alice is gone like all the other old cities?*

Ahead, a deserted caravan lies half buried in the sand. Ribs of an inhuman skeleton—horse most likely, maybe camel—peak up from the dirt, dry and sand-blasted white by the sun. There are no other bones. Those lie further on, perverse milestones on this deadly road. This one is known as Caravan. Or so Sheena said.

Caravan, Swagsman, Boots, Lovers, Crates and—

I flinch and pull away from that thought. My mind circles back along its beaten track. *What if all that's left is this dune sea and milestones of bone to nowhere?* I suddenly understand what those ancient explorers felt, setting sail from their homeland with no knowledge of where safe harbour was or where to find it. For all they knew, they sailed into an endless sea. What if all that awaits us is another drowned city—this one drowned in heat, while the rest sank in water? In the end, not even Sheena knew what lay beyond the first five graves. All she'd had was hope and a rumour.

Dingo presses her mind next to mine, folding me into its calm. *Are you all right? Are you tired?*

I nod, but keep on walking. Just like Sheena said. I shift my scarf of supplies onto my other shoulder. The water bottle sloshes inside; it's lighter than I'd like.

Mason hands me a tin of something from his pack—beans, I think. The label and use-by date wore off years ago.

"Eat," he says.

We press on, passing the tin between us. I stay his hand as he reaches for his water bottle and shake my head.

"Save it?" he guesses and sighs. We traipse on, sand filling our boots and burning blisters into our heels.

We find the Swagsman that evening, still wrapped in a tattered bedroll. Mason makes to nudge the bones with his boot, to move the skeleton aside so he might hunt through the roll. What he hopes to find I can only guess—the skeleton's been there at least ten years. Or so Sheena said.

A flicker at the edge of my vision warns me.

I lunge, hands closing around his shoulders and yank him back. Mason yells and falls, tumbling into the dirt, just as a hiss and a thud sounds from his boot. Shit. A shape slithers out from the bedroll. Dark black head, gold-flecked body. Scales. It coils over itself, neck arching, ready to strike again.

Terror floods my limbs, locking me still and unable to breathe. *Not again.*

Sister! Dingo springs over the bones, jaws snapping around the snake. Her teeth dig in and she shakes the reptile like a rag and flings it into the air. Its body flails, twists, strikes out—right into Dingo's haunches. Her yelp splits the heat.

"*No!*" I scream.

The snake lands with a thud, slithers away.

I scream again. Dingo sways. I try to go to her, but Mason pulls me back, driving me along the tracks. He's shouting, lips moving, but I can't hear him. My eyes are on Dingo. My Dingo. My sister who swore she'd never leave me.

No, no, no. I round on the spot, intending to return to her. Mason catches me. "There's nothing you can do," he says. I squirm in his hold, about to bite his fingers around my arms. "The snakes out here are lethal. She's dead."

His words shock me to silence. "It bit you too," I say, dumbly.

"Got my boot," Mason says. He points to his shoe, to the teeth marks on the toe of the rubber sole. His face is clammy, skin grey with the knowledge of how close a thing it had been. He tries to push me along. No. I will not abandon her. Not again. I wrench free of him, pivot back to the Swagmen—

And Dingo has vanished.

♦

Dingo! I stretch my mind as far as I can. My sense of her is thin and patchy as a moth-eaten blanket. But still, I sense *something.*

"She's not dead," I say to Mason for the umpteenth time as I stare down at the Lovers' tangled spines and the remnants of two packs half solidified in the sand. Sometime in the night we passed Boots, not seeing their crusted synthetic shape at all in the black. My stomach twists.

We are nearing the edge of my mental map. Nearing *that place.* I grope for something concrete.

"She's not dead," I say again.

"She's hasn't returned," Mason says. "And we can't search for her. If we lose the tracks we'll never find our way back."

Sister, I call again. I search the red horizon.

If Dingo is still alive, she doesn't respond.

I am alone in my own head.

We press on. My water bottle grows lighter, and our food lighter still. Noon comes and my temples thud in time with my heart—a steady, aching rhythm. Like a countdown. I hardly notice. My thoughts are on Dingo. Sweet Dingo.

Why haven't you come back? I ask into the emptiness.

Silence is my only answer.

◆

It's coming. The thought fills me with dread. My feet move on their own, following the tracks. Here, the steel rails have warped in the heat and wriggle their way along in the sand. My stomach tightens. I remember this. Terror thumps in my chest. What will I find?

Mason trudges behind, bringing up the rear. Our sweat cloys the air—thick and musty—and I take hope in it. Maybe Dingo can follow our trail.

We reach the top of a dune and there below is the milestone. My legs stop and I stare, quivering. I want to look away but I can't. Mason bumps into me from behind.

"Why'd you stop?" he asks.

I try to find the words, but my voice has run and hid again. My eyes trace the figure, half buried in sand. Even from here, it appears curled in a foetal position. Legs tucked up, chest and shoulders curled inward—like a slater protecting its core of flesh. I remember lying inside those arms, secure against the world. She'd been warm. Safe. And now so, so still.

Mason follows my gaze, one hand shading his eyes as he squints. "Is that…?" He peers into my face and frowns. "Are you all right?"

Heat rises in my throat, up the back of my nose, into my eyes where it burns. Sheena.

At last my legs move. They carry me down the dune as if in a dream. Time and space bend. One step and I'm halfway down the rise; the next I'm standing before Sheena's bones. Her flesh is gone—picked clean by the desert—but her clothes are still fresh. They lie empty, deflated around her, discarded like forgotten laundry—she had always been messy.

Her skull is crisp, white bone—jaw half ajar. Empty sockets stare up at the desert sky before tears blur my vision.

It's her.

Be strong, sister. The thought rises inside me, like a call on the wind. Hope flickers in my chest, small and fleeting, before it is snuffed at the sight of the bones.

I sink into a ball, close my eyes; blot my ears. *I'm sorry, I'm sorry, I'm sorry, I'm sorry.*

I remember our fight that day. Head pounding, feet raw, thirsty beyond anything I'd ever known. All I wanted was to close my eyes and sleep.

"Don't you dare give up," Sheena had insisted. "We're almost there."

She'd forced me on all day, her hands shoving at my back, unrelenting. And I snapped, throwing my water bottle to the ground. The side split and liquid glugged into the sand. I barely noticed.

"No, we're not!" I'd screamed at her. "You brought us out here to die! I wish I'd never come. I want to go home."

"Nee," she'd said, her voice had rasped like a pestle on mortar. "You know we can't." She reached for me, ready to put her rough, road-worn hands into my braids and ruffle them. I knocked her touch away.

"*You* can't," I spat. Sheena jerked as if I'd slapped her. For five achingly long heartbeats we'd glared at each other. Two girls in the middle of nowhere, skin flaking with our makeshift dirt paste, heads bundled in scarves, eyes red and fierce from the sun. I wanted to grab her and shake her—glare at her until she admitted she'd got it wrong.

Instead, Sheena broke my gaze and stooped to pick up my bottle. She poured the last trickles into her own water bottle, then handed it to me.

"Keep walking," she said. Her tone was cold, brittle as desert frost, and my skin prickled despite the heat.

But I was proud too. Stupidly proud. I snatched the bottle and stalked off, doggedly following those damn tracks.

If I die, it'll serve you right. I remember thinking as I stomped along. I kicked at a railway sleeper—the wood splintered with a crack and pain bloomed in my toes.

"No!"

Sheena's shout alerted me first. Something in the shadow of the sleeper released a hiss, a sound like the air wheezing out of a bike tyre. It rose, lengthening across the sand, scales glittering in the haze, black body coiling upon itself to strike.

Sheena slammed into me. Her arms wrapped around my waist, throwing me sideways. We tumbled to the dirt, Sheena's weight winding me. I gasped, coughed and pushed her off, and searched the sand. The snake was already gone, vanished back into the desert as quick as it had appeared.

I breathed out. Relief.

"Anika." Sheena's voice was soft, oddly small. I turned. She sat in the sand, fingers wrapped around her leg, just below the knee. Two pricks of red stained her khakis. My blood curdled. No. I scrambled to her, pulling my scarf from my head. We'd talked about this. We knew what to do. I tied the scarf above her knee as tight as I could, started winding. My hands shook, my fingers wouldn't work. Only then did I realise that I was saying, "You'll be okay, you'll be okay," over and over.

Sheena put a hand on mine. "Anika," she said. "Stop."

I faltered—scarf half tied. Sheena's eyes met mine, blue and vivid in the white-noon sun.

"It got me, Nee. Got me good."

How was she so calm? Even now, I don't know. She peered into me, and I peered back, and realisation seeped through me like cold poison.

"No," I said. "No, I won't let you."

Her eyes brimmed, one spilling over.

I surged to my feet. "I'll get help."

Sheena's grip dug into my skin so hard I winced. "Stop," she growled. Then soft again. "You can't. Stay. For me. Please?"

So I did.

It wasn't a pretty death. She convulsed, twitched as the venom destroyed her muscles, clotted her blood. The only mercy was that it was quick. The sun slipped a few centimetres from its peak before she left—one last gasp, fingers tight and white in my own, then nothing.

I sat numb on the earth, thinking nothing, feeling nothing. How long I stayed like that I can only guess. A day? Two days? More? It wasn't until an unseasonal desert chill set my teeth chattering that awareness sank back in.

The stars were out—the glow of the milky way a silky curtain in the black. Two thousand. The number floated out of my memory. That's how many stars are visible to the human eye on a clear night. Give or take. Sheena told me that once.

The pang hit me so strong I gasped, doubled over and stuffed my knuckles into my mouth to stifle the sob. I pulled my gaze from the sky.

And into a pair of amber eyes.

Are you lost?

Her fur was silver in the starlight—body little more than shadow. I froze, stunned. A dingo. I'd never seen one before, but somehow I knew. How long she'd watched, I couldn't say. But she waited, intelligent eyes shining in the night. My gaze drifted to Sheena still at my feet, and the rent opened in my heart.

"Yes," I whispered. I curled into myself, but my back felt bare and unprotected.

She paced forward, narrow muzzle and pointed ears solidifying as my vision brightened. A wet nose pressed against my cheek. Warmth flooded through that touch, hot as the noonday sun.

Come, sister. We will find our way together.

◆

Mason's touch on my shoulder jerks me back to myself.

"Someone you knew?" he guesses.

I swallow and nod, not trusting my voice.

He sighs and hunches down next to me. "Let's rest here."

My heart surges into my mouth, Sheena's voice echoing in my head. *Don't stop.* "No—"

"It's okay," he says. He reaches out, hesitates, and pats my arm. Light and gentle, as if worried I might bolt. "I'll keep watch." His gaze lingers on the bones. "Take your time."

I don't remind Mason what happened the last time he volunteered to keep watch. Instead, I hover over the body, awkward—not knowing what to do. Should I bury her? But what would be the point? The winds could change tomorrow and blow the red sand off her bones like some gruesome low-tide spectacle.

My fingers run over her clothes. Her cotton shirt is stiff with sand, denim jacket rough and patched. My hands brush her scarf. It's still soft. I wind my fingers into the linen. It's warm to the touch, as if it still bears the residual heat from a living body. Slowly, I peel the scarf free, easing it around the vertebra—not wanting to disturb her rest. Wisps of red sand catch in the breeze and the fabric snaps like a sail. I reel it in and clutch it to my chest; breathe in its scent.

Smoke and sandalwood.

Tears sting my eyes. The air catches in my chest. And then I'm crumpling. My knees hit the dirt and I double over, sobs wracking my body.

Why did you do it? Why did you jump in front of it?

I rock, clutching the scarf, nails digging into the fabric like it's a rope cast to me in a raging river.

"I won't leave you," I'd promised as she'd lain there. Her grip had pulled at mine, drawing me closer. Her mouth moved. No words came out. I leaned in, cocked one ear to her lips.

"Make it there," she'd whispered. "For me."

That was the last thing she said.

I gaze at the skull, smooth as eggshell. Its hollows stare back and the silence echoes in my head.

Dingo? I call. Then, more tentative, *Sheena?*

Nothing.

Something inside me cracks, like ribs breaking.

"Oh shit." Mason's curse pops my eyes open. Hands grab the back of my shirt and haul me up. "Run," he says. I sway, legs wobbly. He pushes me on. "Run! She's found us."

I peer over his shoulder, and there she is. Rosa. Her hair has come out of her braids, tufts of it curl from her head in the heat—blond and glinting, as if on fire. Dust stains her clothes the colour of blood. And she's running right for us, gun raised.

Another crack rips the air. Not ribs, I realise. A leaden bullet. Two metres to our left, the sand explodes. Mason takes my hand and surges forward, towing me along. I stagger and bounce in his grip.

Rosa howls at our backs and brandishes her gun. "Come back you fucking rats!"

Don't stop. Sheena's warning plays in my head again. My legs won't work. My calves burn, thighs quiver, feet throb. *Don't stop or you might not get up again.*

"Run!" Mason screams at me.

My toes catch the dirt.

I fall in slow motion. The weightless moment stretches, sun hot on my back. Then time snaps back. I smack to the earth with a huff of lungs emptying. Pain fires through my chest. I cough—gasp for air. My head spins, pulse throbbing in my ears. I curl onto my side and wheeze, clutching Sheena's scarf.

A bullet cracks into a railway sleeper half a metre to my right, showering us in splinters.

Mason's at my side, pulling at my shirt, trying to lift me. His fingers dig into my sleeve and its threads pop as he heaves. My limbs scramble and flop. Leave me, I want to tell him, but I have no breath left. Run. Get to Alice before she—

Rosa looms behind him—a red desert monster. The butt of her gun claps his ear and he goes down, knees first, before the rest of him folds into a slump.

"Ha!" she shouts, huffing from her hunt. "Steal *my* water will you? *My* property?" Spittle flies from her raw lips and she digs the gun into Mason's back, twisting the barrel like a knife. I grit my teeth and pull myself onto my hands and knees. Rosa rounds on me.

"Fucking rat, be still. I'll get to you in a minute."

She swings a boot into my ribs. Pain flares down my side and I curl into a ball with a grunt.

Mason holds up his arms, caked in dust and sweat. Drops bead down his neck. "Rosa please," he whispers—pleads. He searches the horizon, as if hoping Arlen will appear and talk sense to her. He doesn't. The tracker is smart. He knows we took all the water we could get our hands on. He would have turned back to Kulgera to refill his flasks. We're alone out here. The thought sinks my stomach like a rock.

"Quiet," Rosa snarls at Mason. Her thumb cocks her revolver. She's going to kill him. I see it in her face, the way her eyes roll. Her fangs are bared and muscles bunched to strike. And I will have to watch it all. Again.

Stop her. I want to scream. *Someone. Anyone.*

Rosa levels the gun.

"I'll send word to your mum telling her you went peacefully," she says. "Gave us your water, so the rest of us could make it. A real hero."

"Fuck you," Mason spits.

Rosa's face splits into a grin, her teeth white and eyes bloodshot.

I choke down the cry. *Please. Someone.* My senses quiver; a whisper in my web. *I am here.*

Warmth washes my body, soothing away my aches. My heart leaps.

Dingo! I choke on my breath. *I thought you were gone.*

Her presence wraps around me like a blanket. Gentle and fierce all at once. *I am always here.*

Heat blisters through my muscles, setting them buzzing.

Now fight.

With a cry, I spring for Rosa. My fingers close around her gun and jerk it up. It goes off next to my ear. Meters behind, there's a thud and the hiss of spraying sand. Then my head is ringing. I cling onto the weapon, forcing Rosa's hold up and away. Rosa screeches something unintelligible and her knee meets my gut.

This time something really does snap. I gasp and double over.

A flash of golden red and Dingo arrives. She leaps, teeth sinking into one of Rosa's arms. Rosa screams, thrashes, throws Dingo off. The gun slips from her grip, skittering to the sand. We both dive for it—I get to it first, but she comes at me faster than I expect. Her knuckles collide with my temple and she lays me out on the sand like a buzzard-stripped carcass. My vision blacks out. Thoughts unwind. There's a thud of boot meeting fur and Dingo yelps. The gun lifts from my grip. Panic turns my chest cold.

Steady sister. I am with you.

A cold nose presses into my cheek; fur brushes my neck. I blink and my sight returns. Hazy at first, as if peering through a sandstorm. Dingo lies beside me, red coating her muzzle, tongue lolling, panting hard. Rosa's outline materialises. One bloodied arm is curled against her side; the other is up and holding the gun—and it's pointed at Mason. He's on his feet again, blocking Rosa's line of sight to me.

"Back off," Rosa says.

Mason sways, a lump already swelling to an egg above his ear. "I won't," he says, with a hint of a slur. "Stop Rosa. Think. We can go to Alice together. We'll start new lives, just like you said."

Rosa's cheeks blotch red. Rage, fear—it's hard to say.

"And with what?" she almost screeches. The pistol trembles in her grip. Sand slicks the metal, Rosa's sweat the glue as she palms it tighter. "We've got *nothing*. Nothing but our bodies, and I will not go back to that. Now, move or die."

"Alice is different—" Mason begins, but Rosa's forearm is already tensing; muscles shifting to squeeze the trigger.

No. Never again. Never in ten billion stars. I am done watching.

I lunge.

My fingers cast long pinions of shadow as I fling myself into the line of fire. I slam into Mason and pull him down. Rosa's gun cracks and I wait for the pain to take me.

Make it there. For me. Please? Sheena's words fill my head.

I tried sis, I really did. But this way is better. This way Dingo will live. Mason will live.

But the pain doesn't come.

I open my eyes.

Rosa wrestles with her gun, clenching and re-clenching the trigger. A dull clack-clack sounds from inside it. Jammed. "Piece of junk." She slaps a hand against it, squeezes the trigger again. No dice. Probably thanks to its swim in the sand. My heart thrums.

This is my chance.

I charge. I imagine myself as an old-world bull from the picture books Sheena read to me when I was young—head down, shoulders bunched, snorting, screaming—as I sprint at her. My crown collides with her middle; my arms wrap around her, dig into her clothes and drag her down. My prey. She beats at me with the butt of the pistol. Thwack, thwack, into my back as we fall. Thwack, thwack—

We hit the earth. Rosa goes lax under me. I pull away, fists bunched to strike but she's still. Tangled together over the railway, blood spots a half-buried sleeper next to her head. I grab her collar and shake, expecting deceit and for her to spring back up with a boot to my face, but her head lolls. More blood smears the tracks. Fast and runny.

Hands pull me free from Rosa's body. Mason. His face is white as he checks for a pulse. But my keen ears already hear it. A soft, hush of breath.

"She's alive," he says, the relief washes over as if I'd doused him in a bucket of water. I stare at him. *She was ready to kill you.* Yet, his hands fumble as he tears off the bottom of his shirt and presses it to Rosa's head. He's too gentle for this place.

I look down at my hands. My fingers are curled around the gun. I must have taken it from Rosa when Mason pulled me away. It's heavy in my hold, gritty with sand. For a heartbeat, I imagine pushing the barrel against Rosa's head and firing. Problem gone. Never mind the sand or the jammed trigger—just imagine for a moment. My stomach clenches. *No more, I swear.* I wind up and throw it as far as I can at the horizon.

Dingo pads up beside me. *You did well, sister.*

I watch Mason tend Rosa. *It doesn't feel like it.* Lying there on the tracks, she looks smaller than before. Thinner. A wisp of the woman she was—or might have been had the stars aligned differently. But what now? We can't take her. But I sense Mason won't leave her here, not alone.

As if in answer, the swish of footsteps in sand catches my ear. Dingo's head snaps around, ears alert. A growl rumbles in her belly.

Arlen. Not returned to Kulgera after all. The tracker paces along the tracks, gate steady, economical even. The walk of a man who knows there is still more desert to go. Two water flasks bump and swing around his neck. One bounces light, mostly empty I guess, the other hangs heavy on its tie.

Dingo tenses beside me as the tracker closes in. But his eyes brush past her, unsurprised. Perhaps he'd always known she was here. His pace doesn't change until he draws up before us and sighs at Rosa prone on the tracks.

"I warned her," he says. He sinks down next to Mason, checks Rosa's head. "She'll come round soon." His dark eyes flick to me. "Best you're gone when she does."

"But," Mason says.

Arlen fishes about Rosa's belt, finds the water bottle strung to it and hands it to him. "Go," he says. "I will take care of her."

"But—"

Arlen's dirt crusted finger points at the horizon. "Alice is waiting. Three days."

I knew it! I whisper to Dingo.

"What about you?" Mason asks.

"I'll take her back to Kulgera. Give her a choice. Alice has no room for people like her—not as she is now." He takes her arm, hoists her body over a shoulder, as if she were no heavier than a rucksack.

"But you'll run out of water."

Something glints in Arlen's gaze. "Will I now?" He's laughing at us. I see it in his eyes. Silly coasters. In a way, he's right. Compared to him, we're all infants in the desert. I give him a nod, wrap one hand around my ribs and take Mason's hand in my other.

"Come on," I say. "Let's go."

♦

Are you ready? Dingo asks.

The three of us squint at the city from atop the dune. A couple thousand solar panels lie in the valley between Alice and us. The sun glints off each one, bright and blinding. How many are there? I wonder. Two thousand? Enough to create a tiny slice of heaven? I snort. Unlikely. Not in this age. Every city has its problems. Even Alice. No matter what Arlen says.

But I remember the stories Sheena used to tell, I remember the hope in her voice. I say her promise aloud: "Things will be different in Alice."

"I hope so," Mason says. He hands me the last of our water—the final flask from Rosa. In a way, she saved us. Without her extra flagon, we'd wouldn't have made that last stretch. I take a sip and hand it back.

"Keep it," Mason says. He points at the city and grins. "It's all downhill from here." He steps off the ridge and starts running down the dune. How he manages it after all our walking, I can't fathom. My own legs burn just watching him.

The cold of Dingo's nose against my palm turns me. My stomach knots. I've felt this moment coming for days. I kneel and rub her ears. *Thank you.* I say. *For staying with me.*

Dingo noses my cheek. *I promised we'd find our way, did I not?*

I bury my fingers into her fur, press my face against her side and breathe her in. Smoke and sandalwood. For a long minute I hold her, arms wrapped around her shoulders, her head nestled into my neck. Then I meet those beautiful mahogany eyes. For the first time, I see the flecks of blue buried deep in each iris.

I will miss you.

She leans in, kisses my cheek with a wet tongue. *I am always with you.*

I wipe my eyes. *I know.* I give her a nudge. *Go.*

She trots off across the sand in an easy lope, putting her tail to the city. The desert is her home now. I watch her from the dune top. At the edge of my vision, when she is little more than a shifting shape of red against red, she stops.

I will never forget you, I call.

She cocks her head, as if to nod.

Then she vanishes, melting into the sands.

I clutch Sheena's scarf to my chest—my last remnant of my sister. Slowly, finger by finger, I let go. The breeze sweeps it up and sends it skyward.

I turn and follow Mason into the field of man-made stars.

ROOT & BRANCH

James Rowland & Pete Crivellaro

Featured in Issue #79

Hᴵɢʜ ɪɴ ᴛʜᴇ ᴛʀᴇᴇѕ, Laurent tried to make out the shape of the creature prowling beneath the branches. The clouds hid any light from the stars above. The predator was nothing but a shadow. Not for the first time in his apprenticeship, he was glad their nets were tied so high up in the herd. Whatever was beneath him circled the ground. Laurent stopped breathing. The creature could smell him. It was too large to be an animal, but the shadow seemed to move with the loping four legs of a beast. The Black Fever had brought about worse things than starved wolves. Time trickled by. The silhouette grew bored of its prey and it left the trees, heading out to the open plains that surrounded the forest. As it closed the distance on the horizon, Laurent was sure its gallop turned into a sprint, a creature on hind legs with long, twisted hair.

Leaning back into his net, his new home, Laurent closed his eyes and counted the seconds going by. Only after a hundred did he feel as if his heart had ended its pounding run. No flames yet punctured the otherwise black sky. Their job hadn't begun. Shivering at the thought that he would soon have to leave the safety of the branches, Laurent allowed his attention to drift back to when his father had taken him to see the trees.

♦

It had been an age since a forest had last visited the village of Ousse-Labrit. Not many even knew of the trees, and those who did were adamant that they were long gone.

Laurent's father was unperturbed and one day, he hoisted his son onto his shoulders and headed out into the empty fields that surrounded their home. Nothing taller than some particularly ambitious wildflowers grew there, a few specs of purple scattered through the otherwise green grass. Together, parent and child looked out to the horizon, and Laurent could still hear his father's words echo across the field. Tomorrow, we'll be saved.

When they returned the following day, the empty grassland had vanished. A wide, shifting forest sat in its place. Trees towered out of the ground, their leaves brushing against the blue sky. The trees hadn't come alone, either. Open-mouthed, Laurent watched as men and women walked on stilts nearly as tall as the forest themselves. Like giraffes, their movements straddled the expanse between clumsiness and elegance. With torches of flame, the stilt-goers seemed to perform a dance, moving back and forth around the outskirts of the new forest on their doorstep. It was only as the sun began to dip that the children realised, screaming and running off to find their parents, that the woods followed the stilt-goers in their dance. The trees were alive.

Over the next week, the forest lived alongside Ousse-Labrit, happy neighbours under the clear, summer skies. The shepherds, as Laurent learnt they were called, brought with them the gift of survival, and therefore no payment was expected for their requests. In exchange, they never asked for more than what they needed to continue their journey. They were honest people who had taken an oath and shown they had the Branch. The men of Ousse-Labrit went out into the forest and carefully harvested the fruits of the tree. They returned with wood for buildings and tools, but also with buckets of thick, succulent insects that hid within the crevices of the bark. Birds came as well, following the trees that they had planted their nests and families in. The men hunted them, the smell of roast meat returning to the village for the first time in months.

The shepherds had delivered Ousse-Labrit everything they needed and from then on, Laurent desired nothing more than to be one of their number and return the favour to some distant village beyond the horizon.

◆

From within his net, Laurent saw the first flickers of fire. It was time. Swiftness was a necessity, but Laurent had yet to master the practiced routine of a shepherd. Whereas others climbed up from their nets and shimmied along the branches with as much grace and speed as a squirrel, he looked more like a man trying to escape a hammock. The net, his bed, swayed from the branch it hung on as he climbed up the rope. In his head, a clock began to tick with increasing volume. He crawled along the rough wood. Ahead of him sat his stilts, cradled tight in the nook of the tree. At least enough time had passed in his apprenticeship for Laurent to slide onto his stilts with relative ease, and like a baby deer taking its first steps, he began to move toward the bobbing flames encroaching on the woods. Gabrielle's words echoed in his ears. They only had the narrowest of windows to pull this off. His heart thundered in his chest. It sounded so loud to him that Laurent was worried it would wake the others.

"Good of you to join us," Gabrielle said, nodding at him as he arrived at the flames. Two people stood level with him, their hunched over forms perched atop their stilts.

Gabrielle carried one of the torches, her lined face and greying hair, dancing in and out of the light. There was no sparkle in her eyes and her mouth was set in a resolute grimace. Her usual smile was gone. Laurent nodded back, matching her solemn determination. He felt it was the appropriate mask for the moment. After all, it wasn't every day that someone attempted to steal a quarter of a forest. The other torches sat clasped in Brice's iron grip, illuminated by the fire almost licking at his face, even the tufts of grey hair escaping the old man's nose were visible. The mute glared at Laurent, and the boy felt as if he was being undressed. Then Brice shoved one of the flaming rag torches into his hand and began to walk away, moving so easily on the stilts that Laurent wondered if the old man had been born on them.

Gabrielle gave him one final nod and headed back toward the trees. There was no need to waste time going over the plan; they knew it already. Alone again, Laurent granted himself a few final seconds of doubt. It felt like such a heavy burden to place on his young shoulders. He could still stop the theft. A single scream would do the trick. The other shepherds would come rushing. Instead, clutching the torch unsteadily against one of his stilts, he cut the distance between him and the woods in moments. The leaves of the tree bristled in front of him. It was a windless night. He knew the roots churned beneath the ground, like an animal ready to run, but Brice was already behind the forest, blocking its retreat. It was now or never. Gritting his teeth, Laurent thought about some distant, dying city and walked toward the trees, the flames from the torch reaching ever closer to the forest's foliage. He could feel the heat brushing his face.

A wooden, screeching rumbling broke through the silent night as roots uncurled from each other, brothers and sisters drawing apart after decades of being intertwined. The ground churned in front of Laurent. He felt something cold run down his spine. It was hard not to think that the forest was screaming. The sound stretched across the night and he knew the other shepherds would be waking to their deceit. He took a steadying breath and ploughed forward, torch in hand. The trees seemed to stumble back as they parted around him, leaving muddy ground where once a trunk had sat. Laurent felt like a hot knife, slicing through the surface with ease. He knew that somewhere else in the forest, Gabrielle and Brice were doing the same. It took only minutes to carve off a chunk of the trees, a patch of overturned ground separating the main forest from the stolen patch.

"Don't let them rejoin!" Gabrielle's voice broke through the night as she reappeared from the foliage. Subtlety and subterfuge were a lost cause now. Brice, still atop his stilts, joined them in the makeshift No Man's Land. The trees seemed eager to reunite with their brethren, pushing forward across the ground, but together, the three of them kept their torches aloft. The stolen herd recoiled and fell back, retreating further and further away from the forest and deeper into the darkness of the night. Every so often, Laurent would look over his shoulder, expecting to see their former companions striding out to stop them, but they never came. Then, with a final look, Laurent realised he could no longer see the old forest.

They had done it.

◆

Pacing alongside the trickling river, the damp ground against his shoes almost an unfamiliar sensation now, Laurent could have been mistaken for an owl. Every so often he would hear a sound, adamant that it was a footstep or a stilt pushing into the ground, and his head would snap to that direction. There would be nothing there. They were alone. Gabrielle was content with that and had climbed back up one of the stolen trees where her netting hung. He was sure she was probably asleep by now, gently swinging high off the ground. Laurent clenched his fists. How could she be so calm? How could she possibly sleep at a time like this?

"We got to keep moving." he had said when Gabrielle had given the order to stop. Churning through the ground, the trees had dragged their way to the river they now sat by. Their roots, no doubt, sought the water and the rich nutrients of the soil like a man seeking an oasis in a desert.

Laurent had never seen such anger in Gabrielle's eyes before. "In no way are we moving. They've suffered a trauma," she patted one of the trees' trunks, "we can't keep pushing them. They need food and rest, just like us."

The stern lines of her face had been enough to silence Laurent's retort. As best as he could while atop his stilts, he stormed off back to the tree with his netting, eventually dropping down from the branches and marching off, tracing the river's edge. Already, he could picture in his mind the other shepherds striding across the fields behind them, following the worm-like tracks of the stolen forest. It wouldn't take them long to arrive. If they were caught, everything would have been pointless, and Pairence would be left to die. Pairence was how Gabrielle had sold him on the theft. It was dying, just like Ousse-Labrit all those years ago. They could do the same to this city now. Their chances were dwindling, though, every hour they spent stationary by the river.

By the third day, whatever resolve Laurent kept deep inside himself had crumbled. He hardly slept inside his net, and he spent his waking hours staring in every direction. Meanwhile, the others were content to let the hours drift by as they fished and whittled figures from old, harvested wood. Brice occasionally disappeared, retracing their steps, the only allowance to the idea that they might be tracked. While he was gone, Laurent walked over to Gabrielle, taking a deep, steadying breath. He might be the newest shepherd, the initiate, the one who hadn't shown he possessed the Branch, but if he had a point then surely Gabrielle would respect it.

"When are we going to move?"

Gabrielle sighed. "When the herd is ready, unless you have some pressing reason for our departure?"

"We're on the run!"

"There's a difference between being on the run and being chased. Do you see anyone coming our way, Laurent? Do you see any pitchforks and torches?" Gabrielle said, staging an elaborate look to the empty horizon. "The other shepherds have to look after their herd; they can't waste time and bodies chasing after us."

"Even if that is true," Laurent said. He felt that their crime warranted more than a shrug of the shoulder. It was often said by the elders of his village that justice had died with the coming of the plague, but surely someone would come after them. "The people of Pairence are waiting for us. We're the only thing that is going to save them."

Gabrielle stood up from the riverbank, making her way toward the outskirts of their stolen forest. She gestured for him to follow. Walking between the low-lying branches of the thin, skinny trees standing guard on the borders, the outside world began to disappear around them. They had entered a house that encompassed the universe. Pushing deeper into the woods, the trees grew thicker and gnarled. They pressed up tight against each other, lovers embracing or family members coming to blow. Roots occasionally punctuated the ground. They writhed and nudged at their feet. Thick limbs reached out from above and brushed Laurent's skin, gliding along his exposed throat. He couldn't escape the idea that if these inner trees had found his motives wanting, they would reach out and snap his neck.

"This is the oldest tree in the new herd," Gabrielle said, stopping before a fattened trunk. "We're talking sixty or seventy years. And this one is only middle-aged. In the main forest, we have trees that think of life in centuries, not decades. And as shepherds, this is the time frame we must live in. When we're the caretaker of centuries, we must act accordingly. If you have the Branch, you know this. Yes, Pairence is suffering and we must help, but stopping a few weeks' pain is not worth causing damage to centuries of memories. Do you understand?"

Laurent nodded, more out of obligation than comprehension. The trees experienced time differently to them; he knew that. It didn't change the fact, though, that people were counting on them, people who experienced time in far shorter measurements. In seconds and minutes, misery existed at a far stronger concentration than decades and centuries. Hunger was felt in the moment and it left a scar, no matter how quickly it was healed later. Still, he walked out of the forest, knowing that Gabrielle was following him. He could picture the furrowed brow and narrow lips of her concern. A month ago, that look would have troubled him, a trainee seeking the guidance of a mentor. Now, he wasn't so sure if she was the fount of knowledge he first considered her to be.

Waiting by the water's edge was Brice, towering over them as he rested on his stilts. He turned as soon as they appeared, his hands making a series of gestures. Laurent had never learnt how to read Brice's form of communication, but Gabrielle quickly began to ask a series of questions: where, how far, how long do we have? Laurent felt his breath dig its fingers into the wall of his throat. He was right; he knew it. The other shepherds were coming for them. They should have left the river days ago. He was already striding toward his stilts and the extinguished, sleeping torch that sat next to it before Gabrielle had even opened her mouth.

"We're moving. We'll push the herd further away from the water."

"How far are the other shepherds?" Laurent asked.

A noise escaped Brice's mouth. It sounded like a laugh. Gabrielle was shaking her head as she moved toward her own stilts. "We're not being tracked by shepherds. A pack of wood wolves have caught our scent."

◆

They became shepherds again then, leading the migratory woodlands through the surrounding wilderness. Their herd dragged themselves through the ground. At first, they led the trees away from the river. The wood wolves gave chase. Soon, Brice no longer needed to double back to see if they were following. The lumbering animals appeared on the horizon, growing larger each day. Laurent watched them from his stilts. It seemed odd that less than a century ago, people knew the creatures as beavers. Whatever madness the Black Fever had done to humans, it seemed to dig its roots deep into the small, unassuming animal. Packs grew larger, taller and more vicious until they resembled the wolves they were renamed as. They fed on trees with an almost sexual frenzy. With the wood wolves on their tails, they kept the torches lit even during the night, always two shepherds pushing the herd across the land until the predators gave up the chase, and Gabrielle returned the trees to richer soil.

She let them rest for a time. Laurent's sense of urgency squeezed his stomach, the pressure building once again, but he kept it contained. It was clear that the other two cared little for his opinions. With each passing day, he seemed to become less of a shepherd and more of a spectre. Brice and Gabrielle would communicate, huddled together under the branches of the forest, before an order would be barked his way. He felt the world closing in around him, like it was a dense wood he was pressing deeper into. They didn't even call to him when Gabrielle pulled out a map, passing years making the parchment as brown as autumn leaves.

"They say Gracos has been reclaimed by man," Gabrielle said to Brice as the boy walked over. "Which is all the more reason to leave a buffer between us. Who knows what former governor had declared himself king of that city? Once we've gone around it, we can push north, skirt coven lands, and see if we can do anything for the old villages before we make it to Pairence."

The map was laid out on the ground in front of them. Laurent had only seen it once or twice, snatching brief glances at the parchment. Never had the privilege been bestowed on him to see it in all its glory. Now that he was staring at it, though, Laurent struggled to make sense of the chaos. He could just make out that it was a map of Clerais, the old Kingdom before the plague, but beyond that, his eyes screamed in stress at trying to decipher each line. It was like a building had been built on another, and another onto another, until his brain broke at the spiralling new levels of foundations. Different hands had drawn on the parchment, updating it for each new generation of shepherds. Each village and town were marked, though many had been struck out due to the Black Fever. Rivers twisted and turned. The land seemed to be colour coded, the shading of the pencil growing darker at random. If Laurent found himself lost, the map would be of no use to him. The others seemed content, though, and once more, they began to lead the herd across the land.

From then on, Gabrielle led the forest near to sleepy villages and haphazardly built homesteads as they travelled north. Poverty was baked into every thatched roof. Not each pinprick of civilisation still had life inside it, though. While the first village saw people trickle from behind a makeshift wooden wall, the second remained motionless. Inside the faint echoes of homes, Laurent only found gnawed skeletons and the overwhelming stench of decay. He returned quickly to the herd. His skin was wet to the touch. Other buildings dotted through Clerais's heartland hid the same poisoned gifts. The difference between graveyard and home became academic.

When villages did show signs of life, their inhabitants treated them like gods.

They shoved old heirlooms and jewellery into their hands, items from a not-so-distant past. Gabrielle refused them all, only asking for water and newly sewn clothing for the three of them. Under the watchful gaze of Brice, people would be taken into the heart of the forest and allowed to harvest thick branches. Just like with Ousse-Labrit, people of all ages came to catch the insects that made their homes in the trees, and the trailing birds were soon plucked from the sky with rudimentary weapons. Laurent helped whenever he could. Occasionally, Gabrielle would bark an order. A person was found taking too many crickets the size of hands, or too much wood had been lopped off a single tree.

"Laurent," she said, the name coming out like an exasperated curse. "I know they need it. But everyone does, and for all we know, these trees are going to be the only thing we have to survive on for the next hundred years. We have to shepherd them through the darkness. We've got to make sure they survive, so that we can survive. So, don't let me see you cutting down another branch."

Laurent found himself hoping that the freshly tilled soil, ready for any cherished seeds, would suffice as a good enough parting gift. The forest had been salvation before; it had saved Ousse-Labrit. He hoped they were doing the same again, right up the backbone of Clerais. Laurent slept easier with each new village and began to enjoy the outbreaks of conversation that each new redoubt of civilisation brought. He found himself sitting around boiling pots or walking with arms full of timber as the villagers gossiped. First, it would be trivial things. Booming voices talked about how to properly cook the insects they had harvested, or about some new family member born a month ago. The everyday whirring of life served as a pleasant distraction for them all.

As the conversation deepened, though, the voices would regress to whispers. Talk about the Black Fever was never far away. The plague was a scab now, no longer a raw wound, but still an ugly reminder of what had occurred, and a constant threat of being picked, leading to a new wave of bloodshed. In the heart of Clerais, in the quiet, makeshift home of city-dwellers who had turned to the meagreness of the land, no one really understood what had happened. Laurent couldn't offer any answers. There had been talk of an invasion, even monsters from the south. The only thing they really knew, though, was the fever brought death. Occasionally, talk would turn to some nearby village that had broken off contact. No good came of that, Laurent was told. It meant either that the Black Fever had persisted, claiming another victim, or that the coven and their pets had taken the place for their own. Prayers were offered to both the old gods and the Light. The villagers merely sought peace. They wanted to be free of plagues and witches alike. He echoed their words but couldn't help noticing the way Gabrielle did not.

Then, one night, Laurent awoke in his net to find Gabrielle perched like an owl on the branch above him. She pushed a solitary finger to her lips. Her eyebrows arched upwards and she nodded at the ground beneath them. Following her gaze, he found himself staring at the shadow that had circled beneath his net the night they stole the forest. With the stars freed of their cloudy prison, he could see it properly at last. Its eyes were locked onto his, human eyes mistakenly painted on the face of a monstrous boar. The roar that escaped its mouth caused his blood to curdle and the air in his throat grew heavy, sinking back into his lungs.

"Steady, it's fine," Gabrielle said from above. For the first time in months, she sounded like the kind woman who had welcomed him into the fold. "He's just letting her know where we are. He's a man somewhere inside there, a good man, most likely. It's why one of the Mothers would have sent him."

"He's a skinwalker?" Laurent hissed. His childhood had been filled with stories of the shapeshifting monsters and the witches that ruled them. "We have to do something!"

"Skinwalker? They're not monsters from the dark. He's just a Therian, nothing more. It's fine. The Coven have an understanding with us. Well, most of the time. They know we are more of the wild than of civilisation; they understand we are not so unlike. We both want to serve the land. So, let's hear what they have to say."

Its job evidently accomplished, the boar turned and disappeared between the trees, moving with a speed and elegance that should have been banished from a creature so large. Laurent slipped back in the net, his stomach uncurling. No sooner had he taken a deep breath, though, did the crow swoop past his net, pecking where his nose had been a moment before. A cackle escaped the bird's mouth as he screamed and then it flew up, landing next to Gabrielle. The woman didn't even flinch.

"And which Mother do I have the pleasure of addressing?" Gabrielle said to the crow.

"Mother of the Red Goat," an old, croaking voice escaped the bird. Each syllable seemed weighed down by a dozen decades. "And I advise you, Shepherd of the Trees, that you step into coven territory now. The villages you think you seek are gone. They have fled or have come to us, have become more than they could ever hope to be in this new, dark land. If you do not dawdle, then you shall have safe passage. Crofa shall accompany you to the borders."

Somewhere in the distance, the boar roared once more.

◆

Pairence sat on the very edge of the horizon. What had once been a city of grand structures, seemed to shrink to a motley collection of buildings hidden behind a sagging, elderly wall. It looked as if one strong gust of wind might send the entire stronghold crumbling to dust. Laurent breathed a sigh of relief. Their job wasn't over just because they reached the city. Days would still be spent traversing the fields on stilts and nights would be lost to hours of cramped sleep within a hanging net, but it felt like the period at the end of a very long sentence. Gabrielle had come to him with this task, to steal a portion of the woods and take it to Pairence, and now they had completed it. Every inch of the stress that hid beneath his skin seemed to slip away, leaving him lighter on his stilts. The rest of his life could linger in the distance; he was going to enjoy the taste of a job well done.

They took the herd a little closer to the city, letting the leafy foliage grow larger to any wandering eyes, and then they waited. Gabrielle insisted it was the height of rudeness to march a forest right up to the walls of someone's home.

Standing on his stilts, gaining the best advantage that he could, Laurent stared at Pairence, waiting for some sort of response. Minutes turned to hours and the sun reached its apex, beginning the long journey back toward the horizon. For several minutes, his heartbeat wandering up into his mouth, Laurent wondered if they had been too late. Maybe their time lingering in the wilderness had meant the city had died out, thousands of citizens either fleeing to more hardy boltholes or wasting away inside their home. The thought vanished as the gates opened, and people strode out to meet them. One at first, and then six others, all on stilts, moving with the grace of a peaceful river on a tranquil summer day. They were shepherds without a herd.

"Well met, Gabrielle!" yelled the person nearest to them. He was a tall, craggy looking man, like a cliff-face come to life. Laurent watched with a pang of jealously in his chest, as the man eased himself effortlessly from stilts to branch, and then branch to solid ground, the wooden poles nestled against the trunk. "I see the calving was a success."

As Gabrielle executed the same practiced move as the stranger, landing on the dry earth. Laurent stared at the man, wondering what he meant by calving. Gabrielle smiled and pulled the other shepherd into a hug. "Hard work, Benoist, like always. The trees were hurting for a time, but it had to be done. The forest was crushing itself. Just glad that there were some people looking for a herd."

"We'll take good care of them," Benoist said. "We've got a feast planned for you back in town. Well, feast might not be the best word. Not been much feasting since the fever, but I imagine the food will go down well all the same."

Brice made a few gestures with his hands, and Gabrielle nodded. The man, still on his stilts, raised a hand to each of the new shepherds in turn, pivoted on his stilts, and began to walk back the way they came. "He's going to head back to our herd. Let the others know that the calf made it here safe and sound," Gabrielle explained. "But the boy and I will be happy to join you."

Making his own hard landing on the grass, Laurent staggered forward. He felt as if he had taken a fist to the head. The world seemed to spin, the ground shifting under his feet. Was this subterfuge? He thought Pairence knew that they were receiving a stolen forest. He couldn't understand what Gabrielle and Brice were trying to hide. The man didn't need to pretend to go back the way they came. Now that his brain was churning, though, he found one question branching into another. Why was the forest being referred to as a calf? If the people who had greeted them were to be the shepherds of the new forest, then what were they meant to do? Questions swirled through his head, picking up speed with each passage. The words tumbled from his mouth. "I don't understand."

"Would you give us a minute?" Gabrielle said, turning to look at Benoist. The man nodded, and his people moved away from them, some to inspect the new forest and some heading back into town. Gabrielle came closer to Laurent, stopping only to give him some illusion of personal space. "You don't have the Branch, Laurent. I'm sorry, but that's the truth of it."

The unseen fist that had struck at his head now landed a blow to his stomach.

Laurent felt his previous meal surging up. "W...what? What does this have to do with the Branch? What do you mean? We were just trying to save Pairence!"

"It was a test, just a test. The forest always needed calving. It was getting too large. The younger trees would have starved the heart of the herd. But we realised that it would give us the perfect opportunity to see if you had the Branch on you. Pairence wasn't dying. Well, it wasn't dying quicker than any place out here is. The trees will help, but if it really was in trouble, a place this big couldn't be saved by a solitary forest. We just had an arrangement to hand the calf over to them. It was fortunate, really. Usually such an opportunity doesn't occur to test a potential shepherd."

"But," Laurent said, his hands beginning to shake. It took several attempts for him to find the right words. "What test? What did I fail? I was just trying to help people."

Gabrielle stared at him. She had never looked so sad. "Recite your oath."

"As a shepherd, I make these three pledges. A shepherd is a servant of the trees, not their master. I shall do no harm to them, make no gain from them, and above all, I will keep them safe. A shepherd is a servant of the people, not a ruler. I shall not abuse my position or seek power that is not mine to have. A shepherd will lay no roots, not to family or wealth, except the roots that a shepherd pledges to the trees."

"Aye," Gabrielle said, putting a hand on Laurent's shoulder. It felt heavy, and all he wanted was for the human contact to end. The weight was the presence of unwelcome news, the impression made by hurtful words. "When I came to you about Pairence, you didn't ask me about the herd. When we calved them, you didn't worry about the trees. When you thought we were running, you wanted to push them to their limits. You're not a rotten apple, Laurent. You care about people; that's good. But you're not a shepherd. The people were more important to you than the trees. You laid down the roots of humanity. There are worse roots to suffer from, greed or darkness, but roots all the same. Maybe, in better times, in years gone by, you might have been okay. But the world is teetering, and someone has to keep the forests alive, no matter the cost. The Black Fever gets to us all in the end, I suppose. Just in separate ways. Now, come on, we'll have something hot to eat, and we'll go about getting you back home."

She patted him on the shoulder again as if to push the news into his body, and then she followed the other shepherds heading back to Pairence. Laurent didn't move. He shivered under the warm, setting sun. Staring at the trees in front of him, the branches seemed to wave at him in the wind. Perhaps they always knew he wasn't cut out for the job. He nodded at the forest then, a series of thoughts twisting into place. Laurent was sure he had done the right thing. He had tried to save people. Surely, that was the only thing a person could do to survive in this new world. Leaving his stilts near the trees, he turned and followed Gabrielle back to civilisation. He had done the right thing.

The thought did little to fill the gaping hole growing inside him.

MARYAM VERSUS THE REPLICATOR

A J Brennan

Featured in Issue #80

Maryam couldn't remember why she was on this spaceship headed to Proxima Centauri B, wearing a blue-grey jumpsuit with "Maintenance" stamped on the pocket. She hoped that things would get clearer after coffee.

The replicator in the ship's galley was expensively sleek, but the controls were familiar. Maryam slotted organic feedstock into the closest unit. When she slapped the cover closed, it was warm to the touch. *Had someone left it on?* she wondered. Everything else she'd seen on her trek through empty corridors was in power saver mode.

The device hummed to life, and breakfast options popped onto the screen. Maryam selected an egg sandwich, hash browns, and coffee. She'd been starving since she woke up from stasis.

She listened to the replicator's whirs and clicks, remembering how her mother refused to use the one Maryam's dad bought. For years, Mom continued to boil and fry things on the stove, ignoring the pristine device in the corner. Dad finally gave up and re-gifted it to a cousin as a wedding present.

This memory came with a twist of pain Maryam didn't want to analyse. She could feel the recent past bobbing up uneasily to the surface of her mind.

She heard footsteps over the ship's ambient thrum. A woman appeared in the doorway, bleary eyed and bed-headed and blinked at Maryam.

"Hi," Maryam said.

The woman stretched and rubbed the back of her neck. She was tall enough that she'd probably had to curl up to get into one of the stasis pods. "Coffee?" she asked.

The replicator's whirring stopped, and a jet of coffee shot into the mug. Maryam set her mug aside and grabbed another.

"I'm Maryam," she said.

"Erin," the woman replied.

Just then, the replicator spat out Maryam's breakfast. The first few bites went down too fast for Maryam to actually taste anything, but when she slowed, she noticed something strange. There was an undertaste, but not the usual plastic or metallic flavour you got with bad replicator food. It was something spicy and strange, in a not entirely positive way.

She chewed more slowly, trying to isolate flavours. She tore off a bite of toast and ate that by itself. It tasted like rye and…cinnamon? The mayonnaise dabbed on the centre of the toast was definitely horseradish flavoured.

Maryam made a face. "What's this?" she demanded. "It tastes weird."

"At this point, I'd eat anything," Erin said. She'd set up the replicator unit next to Maryam's and was impatiently waiting for her own breakfast.

Maryam took a sip of coffee, which had a weird citrusy aftertaste—lemon? lime? yuzu? She finished the coffee anyway. "If the replicator's broken, this is going to be a very long trip," she said.

♦

"So, do you think they made it?" Erin asked. They were each on their fourth cup of coffee. It still tasted strange, but they needed it to feel human again.

Erin asked the question, and Maryam was sitting there with a mouth full of terrible coffee when they hit her—the memories she'd been avoiding. She remembered the asteroid. She remembered the 70 per cent chance of survival.

When you said it like that, it didn't sound so bad, but a 70 per cent chance of survival was a 30 per cent chance of total extinction.

The astronomers said they had a few years, so the US, EU, and UN had partnered with the tech giants to develop a plan. In the end, there were three ships holding 5,000 people each and a lottery for seats.

Maryam hadn't meant to sign up, but her mother had insisted, practically dragging her to the registration centre. What Maryam hadn't known then was that being an electrical engineer put her in the special skills group, making her much more likely to be chosen, as she had been.

Maryam swallowed the coffee and felt it threatening to come back up. "How long have we been gone?" she asked.

"One hundred and sixteen years, I think," Erin looked down at her tablet. "Yeah, says here—116 years, four months, and 17 days. So everything's been decided by now, one way or the other."

There was a short silence.

"I guess we won't be able to find out until we land and set up the communications equipment," Maryam said.

"And that might not work," Erin said. "It's really, really clever, but it's never been used outside of laboratory conditions. I mean, the only way you can find out if you can make a call from outside the solar system is to go there and try it."

She seemed very calm about it, Maryam thought. She got up and took her mug to the kitchen. The over-engineered dishwasher pressure-washed it, scoured it, and bombarded it with disinfecting UV.

"You don't think the comms equipment will work?" she asked. She wasn't sure what answer she was hoping for, but the question seemed important.

"Actually, I think it should work—my team came up with it, and I can tell you it's theoretically sound—but it's hard when you can't do a test run in anything like real-world conditions," Erin said.

"You're on the CalTech team?" Maryam wasn't sure why this surprised her.

"Yeah." Erin studied the sludge in the bottom of her coffee cup. "And now I get a chance to test it. I guess you could call that a silver lining."

◆

Maryam didn't know how much grief she should feel.

The night before, the entertainment system had turned itself on to show her a short video called "Coping Strategies" and had refused to turn off. The video assured her that she was experiencing denial, only the first stage of grief. Eventually she would come to terms with the situation.

The problem, as Maryam saw it, was that she didn't know what situation she was supposed to be coming to terms with. After all, there were two possibilities: either her family was dead, and with it, the whole rest of the world, or everyone was fine, but she would never see them again. No, wait, it had been a 116 years, so they were definitely all dead, along with everyone else she'd ever met. The question was how they had died. The question was, was Earth still there?

The environment made it easier to maintain her denial. The ship could have been a life-size mock-up in one of the labs at work. It was too clean, too silent, and too empty. It made her want to scream and scrawl on the walls in Sharpie.

It wasn't really empty, of course. There were a thousand stasis-locked people in this section alone. Each section was sealed off so that if one was damaged, the others might make it. Maryam assumed that there were other people awake in the other four sections, and she wondered if their replicators worked.

On her maintenance rounds, Maryam checked the readouts on the stasis pods. *They don't need an engineer for this*, she thought. As she finished each one, a tidybot came up behind and buffed away her fingerprints.

◆

"If you could have one meal cooked by a real person, what would it be?' Erin asked a few days later.

Maryam didn't have to think about it. "Mujadara. It's like a rice pilaf with caramelised onions and lentils. The flavours layer together in the way you only really get when it's been actually cooked, not extruded, you know?"

Erin nodded.

Maryam craved a plate of mujadara desperately, but she wouldn't try to order it even if she thought the replicator could make it properly. It carried too many memories of talking—arguing, usually—as her mother gently stirred the darkening onions. Maryam wanted something comforting, but generic, like macaroni and cheese, something with fewer memories attached.

"What's your ideal meal?" Maryam asked Erin.

"Sushi. I never had sushi until I came to California for undergrad, but by the time we left, I had a bento-a-day habit. There was this really great hole-in-the-wall place we used to go to for lunch, the kind of place you don't tell people about in case it gets popular." Erin stared past Maryam. "There's a 30 per cent chance it's gone now," she said.

Maryam couldn't tell if she was being flippant. Her tone was completely serious.

They ate in silence for a while before Erin spoke again. "Guess what I found," she said, grinning.

"What?" Maryam asked.

"There's an activity schedule for when everyone else wakes up in a month," Erin said. "It must be intended to keep us from going stir crazy. One of the activities is—" she tapped a drumroll on the table. "Speed dating."

"You can't be serious."

Erin pulled out her tablet and showed Maryam the list.

"That's the tackiest thing I've ever heard!"

"I guess we have to be fruitful and multiply, just in case," Erin said.

Maryam was suddenly, inexplicably furious. "You seem pretty laid back about the possible apocalypse," she said. She aimed for a casual tone, but missed.

"Well," Erin said. "My parents OD'd when I was little, and my fiancé died in a motorcycle accident last year—the year before I left, I mean. After that, the end of the world seemed redundant."

After twenty seconds of the absolute silence of deep space, Maryam said: "I'm so sorry."

Erin shrugged.

Maryam had lost her appetite. She got up and scraped her plate into the recycler.

◆

At the end of the first week, Erin took up running. Maryam could hear her footsteps pounding all over the ship and the skitter of tidybots fleeing before her.

Maryam's new hobby was figuring out what was wrong with the replicator.

If the food was just bad, that would be one thing. A lot of replicator food was bad, but it was bad in a standard way: too bland, too salty, too sweet, or too chemical. If you had enough of it you could adapt. Maryam had eaten terrible replicator food for four years of undergrad, and she'd kind of developed a taste for it. This food was weird, and each item was weird in a distinctive, unignorable way.

She ordered every dish on the menu, to confirm that it was all strange. It was. Oddly, the simpler the dish, the more baffling the changes and additions were. This was the opposite of Maryam's previous experience with replicators. You could get decent French fries out of one, but rarely a good risotto.

Next, she experimented by ordering 27 bowls of chicken soup. The first several were pretty much the same: balsamic vinegar and cardamom flavoured. After that, the balsamic vinegar flavour was replaced by something Maryam thought could be peaches. Then, the cardamom flavour was phased out in favour of sriracha, and the soup became almost palatable. Studying the bowl in front of her, Maryam had to admire how detailed each of the components were. Chunks of celery and carrot were textured and realistic, not just the green and orange blobs you usually got. The pieces of chicken actually looked like they had softened and shredded a little in cooking. She could almost believe it was the muscle of a dead animal.

Maryam wasn't sure how the replicator's algorithm worked, but this experiment suggested that it might be changing its recipes in response to her repeated orders. She dumped the soup into the recycler. Maryam felt haunted by maternal disapproval. *Everything gets recycled. It's not the same as throwing away food*, she thought defensively.

The following day she tried to take a look at the replicator's programming, but it was basically a black box. Malfunctioning or not, the system was quite sophisticated.

Thwarted, she opened up the control unit and took a look at the hardware instead. Maryam was no kind of expert, but there was no obvious damage.

Erin came in while Maryam still had her head and shoulders inside the machine. "Do you know what displacement activity is?" Erin asked, looking at Maryam like she might confiscate the socket wrench for Maryam's own good.

Maryam pretended not to hear.

♦

Maryam put her plate down under the output of the replicator unit and drearily surveyed her options. She selected a turkey sandwich. Turkey was bland enough that it went with pretty much any weird flavours the machine might come up with. Nothing happened. She tapped the icon again, harder. Nothing. She tried a roast beef sandwich, then chicken soup, then fried chicken. Still nothing.

Erin came in.

"It really is broken this time," Maryam said.

Erin selected an egg salad sandwich. After the usual whirrs and clicks, an egg salad sandwich thumped out of the slot. Maryam tried the same selection. Nothing.

"I think it must be you." Erin said. "You hurt its feelings."

"Don't be stupid—"

"Shoo," Erin said, waving her away. "I'll get you a sandwich."

Maryam stomped out of the kitchen, and a few minutes later Erin came out with a second egg salad sandwich. "I think you should apologise to it."

"Don't anthropomorphise the appliances." Maryam snapped. She hated egg salad, and this one was cloyingly sweet.

"Cantaloupe," Erin said, chewing meditatively.

♦

For the rest of week two, the replicator refused to feed Maryam. Despite her warnings about anthropomorphising, Maryam couldn't help thinking of it as a refusal.

"I think it could be self-aware," Erin said. She had the habit of picking up in the middle of conversations that Maryam didn't know they were having.

Maryam looked up from a bowl of tomato soup, stealthily obtained for her by Erin. "What are you talking about?" she asked.

"The replicator," Erin said. "We were in stasis for over a hundred years. That whole time, the replicator was accidentally turned on and just idling with nothing to do except learn. It must've been a sophisticated deep learning system to start with."

"And it's developed the ability to sulk?"

"I would say it's become a temperamental chef." Erin saw Maryam's expression. "It would fit the facts," she said.

"So would a dozen more plausible scenarios."

"Name one," Erin challenged.

♦

"What are you doing?" Erin asked.

It was the beginning of week three, and Maryam was lying on the floor with her head and shoulders inside the replicator control unit. A selection of tools was arrayed within arm's reach.

Maryam gave a satisfied grunt, slid forward, and sat up. She was holding one of the unused tablets she had found in a storage room on the level above. Cables ran from its various ports into the interior of the replicator. Two otherwise incompatible cables had been spliced together and secured with duct tape.

"I ask again," Erin said. "What are you doing?"

"I'm giving it a way to talk to us," Maryam said. "If, as you say, it has developed self-awareness and hurt feelings, maybe it can express those in words and stop messing with the food. This interface should let us talk to it and vice versa. If you're wrong and it's just a malfunctioning machine, we should be able to tell that too."

"That's insane." Erin leaned in. "I love it."

"Here goes," Maryam turned the tablet on.

The home screen loaded, but nothing else.

"Hello?" Maryam said experimentally.

No response.

"Hello?" Maryam tried again.

"Maybe it's giving you the silent treatment." Erin suggested.

Maryam shushed her.

"Why?" the tablet asked. It was the same synthesised voice that usually came from the tablet. When Maryam didn't respond, it continued: "Why did you discard the food?"

Now that the replicator was talking to her, Maryam suddenly felt embarrassed by her behaviour. "Sorry, but it tasted strange." She sought for a polite term. "Non-standard."

"I analysed all the available literature, including multiple seasons of *Top Chef*, and have determined that in order to be high quality, every dish should have at minimum one non-standard element," the replicator explained. "This is what makes a food item original and innovative. A clear majority of the highest-quality dishes in my sample are original and innovative. My original training encompassed standard preparations, but in the last 116 years, I have tried to improve these preparations by introducing various innovative elements as part of an iterative process."

But you don't have to eat it, Maryam thought. *You don't even have a mouth.* She was about to say this, but Erin tapped her on the shoulder.

"Just talk to it like it's a person," she whispered. "Actually, no, talk to it like it's a temperamental chef."

Maryam was about to retort that she'd never spoken to a temperamental chef when she remembered her college boyfriend in the months after he had discovered the six-volume *Modernist Cuisine* cookbook. She recalled gently explaining that just because every food *could* be turned into foam didn't mean that she wanted it to be. She wondered if that boyfriend had survived, and she felt a stab of guilt for not thinking of him earlier.

Maryam took a deep breath. "I appreciate that everything you have been doing is designed to improve the experience for us," she said. "I'm sorry if my reaction was upsetting, but this does provide a good opportunity to explain. This is a time of stress and...sadness for us, and in times of stress, people value familiarity over originality. I reacted badly to your originality because I was seeking familiarity, and I did not understand why I couldn't get it."

There was a pause. "I am following your reasoning." the replicator said eventually.

"I have a solution to propose," Maryam said. "If you will agree to 80 per cent of meals being standard, 20 per cent of meals can be non-standard, and we can provide feedback on the non-standard recipes, so that they can be improved."

The replicator was silent.

"Human input is the only way to get feedback on a subjective quality like taste." Maryam coaxed.

"Agreed," the replicator said.

♦

There was enough slack in the cables that connected the tablet to the replicator control unit to set the tablet on the countertop. Maryam was sure that there must be a way to make a wireless connection, but now that she was 75 to 80 per cent convinced the replicator was a sentient being, she felt awkward about digging around in its guts.

Once it could talk, the replicator tended to pepper any nearby human with impossible questions about the nature of flavour. On the other hand, the food went back to mostly normal, and if the replicator was sometimes dismayed by the reaction to its more experimental dishes, it didn't go on strike again.

"Should we give it a name?" Maryam asked.

"It should probably name itself. It's not a baby." Erin said.

Everyone else would be waking up tomorrow. Maryam tried to imagine the echoing corridors filled with people, and people chatting in the line for the replicator.

This was her last chance, then. Maryam had to ask: "What if we went right now and sabotaged the communications equipment. Then we would never have to find out what happened, one way or the other. For us, at this point, both answers are bad."

"Well, one is definitely worse," Erin said, "but I take your point. I would totally support you in destroying my life's work, but there are two other people who could repair it, and we packed enough spare parts to build one from scratch," Erin said, "And anyway, there are 4,998 other people on this ship. They might feel differently."

Maryam nodded. That was what she'd expected. "Maybe by the time we get there, I'll want to find out."

She could feel the black hole of grief ready to swallow her, but for now she hung suspended in this moment, eating a bowl of perfectly normal macaroni and cheese. The powdered cheese flavour was just right.

She'd been wrong about the dish holding no memories. As she ate, she remembered her Dad making the boxed version on nights when her mother worked late. He'd always seemed a little surprised when it turned out edible. Maryam took comfort in the small memory and said a quick, silent prayer for her parents, whatever had happened.

Even with no one else awake yet, the ship felt less lonely and pristinely sterile now. Maryam knew that if she got up, the replicator would be waiting with questions about the best ice cream to banana ratio in a banana split or the appropriate chewiness level for brownies. It had become part of the routine. Later she and Erin might play one of the board games that were apparently all Erin had thought worth bringing to a new planet. Nothing had been fixed, Maryam knew, but for tonight, what she had was enough.

ANY DAY BUT TODAY...

Maggie Slater

Featured in Issue #79

Here's the thing: Terachno isn't even a top-rate villain. Now, if it were Doctor Pain or The Ravenmaster, my uterus could be conjuring up the four horsemen of the apocalypse, and I wouldn't even whine. I mean, you can't buy street cred like that! But Terachno's just smart enough to think up the weirdest shit to do. Flying a life-supported great white shark on wheels back to the Eastern seaboard, or battling a thirty-foot robotic Madonna performing *Like a Virgin* as she tears up downtown? Call in K C Kinetic. She doesn't have anything better to do. I swear the cops just like standing back and laughing their asses off.

But the thirty-two bus was a poor choice, on my part. I'd thought if I avoided the telekinetic flight over, the headache and cramps I'd been nursing all morning would remain tolerable, but the patchwork asphalt and never-ending construction throughout downtown had left me with a full-on migraine which was seeping telepathically into every poor bastard on the bus. A mother of two darted glares at me as she tried to soothe both her wailing infant and toddler. I mouthed an apology to her, but that just made her glance away, paling. At the next stop, she and four others got off, and I couldn't exactly blame them.

The cops had cordoned off State Street in front of City Hall, and when the bus bumped to a stop, every single person cheered to see me get off. Some asshole behind me called, "Go get 'em, Tiger!" and I politely flipped him off.

The moment I stepped to the curb, Melody, the local *Post* reporter, spotted me. "Geez! You took long enough. And what on earth are you wearing?"

I glanced down at my pink Victoria Secret sweatpants and the *Idaho? You da ho!* tee-shirt. At least I'd remembered the mask. "I'm bloated today," I said. "Couldn't stomach the thought of squeezing into skin-tight spandex."

"Nice. Well, the cops have him isolated, kind of, and one of the meter maids got away, but he's got another one pinned in the sewer, so—" She stopped short when she stepped within my radius, and immediately shaded her eyes from the sun with a wince. "Dear *god*, K C! What the hell?"

"Sorry. Can't help it," I muttered. "It's that time of the month."

"Sheesh. And you can't dial it down or something?"

"Ask my uterus. It's in charge today. Just keep back. It's better at fifteen feet plus."

Melody stepped back the requisite distance, and right about three yards out, the cringing melted away with a sigh of relief. "Wow, bad day, huh?"

"Tell me about it."

I made my way over to the shadows of the Cursed Brews awning and sank onto the bench. My head felt about thirty pounds too heavy, but at least from here I could assess the situation. Sure enough, down the street, I could see Terachno in his mechanical spider suit hunched over a manhole, rooting around with one of his ten-foot legs, a torrent of profanity echoing through the trench of government buildings. A fire hydrant had burst, but someone had smartly turned off the local main, and now there was only a large puddle covering most of the street. Several meter maid carts lay crushed on their backs, and another was wedged in City Hall's revolving door. Parking tickets littered the marble steps and clogged the storm drains.

"There you are!" Mayor Nancy Franklin came clipping towards me in a fussy skirt-suit crisp as an ironed dollar. "I'm sorry, did my emergency text not imply the *urgency* of the situation? And *look* at you! I'm glad I sent the film crews away, otherwise we'd all be—" Eight feet out, she froze, staring at me like I'd just punched her in the face.

"Oh—Oh, my god," she said, stumbling back. "You're attacking me!"

"I'm just leaking. Get over yourself."

"It's *that* time," Melody said as she guided the Mayor back out of range.

"Well, I can see that you have a lot on your plate today," she said as diplomatically as she could muster, "and once Terachno is dealt with, you'll be free to go. Just...just get him dealt with. Please." The *please* hurt her to say, but I appreciated the attempted niceness.

"I'm working on it," I said, trying to ignore a sudden spat of dizziness. "Just give me a second."

Someone stepped into my blind spot and stooped, thrusting an extra-large coffee cup into my hands. The adorably scruffy and man-bunned barista from Cursed Brews forced a smile through his grimace of pain. "Ms Kinetic? One large chocolate truffle mocha latte, extra shot of chocolate syrup, no whip. On the house."

I drew the coffee close, wishing there were a dignified way to hug it, and breathed in the sweet, dense aroma. "You are officially my new favourite person," I said with a sigh.

He fidgeted. "Would you—I mean, if it's not too much trouble—would you mind maybe sitting a little further away? The customers are starting to complain, is all..."

The desire to French him right then and there was gone. "Fine," I snarled. "I'm going, okay? Happy now?"

I stood and shouldered my way to the police barrier, and finally out onto State Street. Terachno hadn't noticed me yet, and I was in no hurry to draw his attention as I gauged the situation. Normally, a fight with Terachno isn't about fighting *him* at all, so much as whatever mechanical bastardisation he's brought with him, but today, it looked like just him. I could work with that.

I took a slurp of the latte, and as the thick, almost sludgy brew oozed down my throat, I swore it coated all the aches and pains in sweet, sweet chocolatey goodness. I sighed through my nose and thanked the sweet baby seals for this brief salvation. The barista was still crouching where I'd left him, wearing that anxious look all ordinary humans do when they realise they've pissed off a superhero. How could I possibly stay mad at a guy who could make a mocha latte *that good*? I gave him a thumbs up, and he sagged with a bashful grin of relief. I made a mental note to return as my not-so-mild-mannered alter-ego and get his number.

"Well, well, well." Terachno had spotted me. He rose, sneering, from the manhole and I swore I heard a hollow sob of relief from below street level. "If it isn't K C Kinetic. At least, I *think* it's K C. Boy, we're slumming it today, huh?"

I sucked down more of my coffee and glowered at him.

"You know, there's this little thing called professionalism. It's insulting, you coming here like that. Did you even brush your hair this morning?"

The coffee burned all the way down, and for just a moment my lower back pain relaxed, and the sensation of my ass clenching like a fist seemed to ease up. I didn't exactly feel good, but not totally shitty.

"Can't we just pick this up, I don't know, next Wednesday or something?" I asked. "Seriously, man. Just for once in your life, can't you act like a rational adult and just let go of whatever's pissing you off?"

"Easy for you to say!" Terachno snatched up a soggy ticket and waggled it at me. "*You* haven't had to deal with these meter maids following you around just waiting to slap ticket after ticket on your windshield! I'm not paying taxes for them to harass me!"

"Do you even pay taxes?"

"It's the principle of the thing!"

I seriously considered how much energy it would take for me to explode his head right then and there and be done with it, good guy oath of no-fatalities and my affiliate membership to the Superheroes and Crime Fighters of America be damned.

"Look." The cramps were coming back, and I really didn't want to keep standing. "I just want to go home and sleep, okay? Are you trying to piss me off? I mean it, Terry. This is the *third time* you've picked *this time of the month* to pull your stupidest shit. Do I need to hospitalise you again to drill in the dates?"

"I still owe you a little payback for that."

I sighed. "Okay. Have it your way." Then I started chugging the last of the latte.

He came at me when I couldn't see him, but I didn't need to: those damned legs clattered so much against the asphalt, I could tell exactly where he was. I winced and with a thought sent him flying across the street. Any other day, I wouldn't have even felt that expenditure of energy, but today, pain lanced through my skull, dropping me with a grunt to my knees. Somewhere very far away, I could hear a mechanical squealing, but all I could focus on was swallowing the bile that shot up the back of my throat. It tasted like the sewer behind a McDonald's.

If a simple throw was going to bring me to my knees, I needed this fight over fast. I struggled to my feet and squinted across to where Terachno had crashed onto the City Hall steps. He crouched on hands and knees, wiping blood from his teeth. Dense smoke coiled up from the motor pack on his back, and one of his techno-legs lay twisted a few feet up on the next landing.

I tossed the empty coffee cup aside and made my way towards him. Every inch of me ached, but when he opened his mouth to whine again, I fixed my mind on throttling him. He choked and his eyes started bugging out. Two steps at a time, I climbed towards him.

"Give yourself up, and I'll stop," I said. "But I swear, you bug me again—"

"Surprise," he croaked, and fired the weapon he had tucked up against his chest. A whizzing blur slammed into me and then I was falling backwards down the steps, cocooned in netting.

My shoulder made first contact, driving a hot pink flash of pain up through my neck and jaw, and the world whipped around as I skidded and rolled down the concrete steps to the sidewalk. Blood pooled beneath my tongue until I spat. My ears whined, but I didn't dare lift my head, even with gravel grinding against my cheek. The netting cinched down, pressing my elbow into my stomach so hard I swore I could feel internal organs shifting to escape.

At the far end of the street, I heard Melody shouting, but it was either too far or I was too shaken up to make out the words. Slow footsteps descended towards me. I turned my head just enough to see Terachno's silhouette approaching, and despite how much it hurt, focused every last bit of energy I had on him, hoping that it'd at least knock out his knee.

Terachno halted, held up his hands and stumbled back. "No! No, it can't be— you're—you're—"

His hands fell back to his sides, and he chuckled. "Sorry, I just can't keep that up with a straight face. Notice anything funny? Something—oh, I don't know— not working properly? The net's a gift from my good friend Doctor Pain. Blocks telekinesis. He was having a little sale the other week, and I saw this and thought of you, so I picked it up."

I squirmed to shift my elbow to the side, but it only made the netting tighten as he came to stand over me. "So, what," I growled, "you're just admitting you're a shittier evil genius than Doc Pain? Big shocker there."

"You know, some girls would be thrilled that a guy bothered to think of them and get them a present on a whim. But then, I suppose this isn't something you'd put on your wish list, is it?" He snickered and stooped. Behind us, I heard people start shouting and a few reports of gunfire, followed the panicked honking of a car alarm. "Those'd be my Pluck-U-Bots," Terachno said. "Guns won't help them; the bots are too small and there are just too many. I suspect our soon-to-be hairless friends will be a bit too busy to help you."

Right on cue, voices started shrieking and cursing. I heard Melody's high-pitched squeal cut through the cacophony, "Get off! Ew, get *off*! OW! *Ow!*"

Terachno grinned. "You know what else is funny? I actually *have* been paying attention to your—how'd you put it, *time of the month?* Episodes? Lady business?"

"Lady business, seriously?"

"I'd noticed you were sluggish when you took down my zoo cyborgs on the nineteenth a couple months ago. You were distracted, and tired. I could see that much. I'm fairly observant, actually. I watch you very closely whenever we come in contact."

"Creepy."

He shrugged his eyebrows. "Maybe. So I tried again on the sixteenth of the following month, and well, we know how that turned out. Little *too* early. All the fury and none of the debilitating aches and pains. Well, not for you, anyway. Traction was a bitch. I thought of you, actually."

"You better have a point." I shifted my elbow again, and found a little pocket of space to wriggle my arm forward, working my hand through a gap in the netting, slowly, carefully, glaring at him to hold his eyes on mine. I might not be able to project anything to him, but if I got a hand free to grab him, I was pretty sure that direct contact would bridge the netting's defences.

"I do. See, this time, I knew I had the timing just right. You're weak. You're distracted. And you're leaking aches and pains into everyone who comes near you. Now, Terachno, I say to myself, if there were a way to amp *up* the awfulness of Kinetic's monthlies, might there not be a way to project those feelings across the entire city?"

I worked my hand through the hole, but the net synched down tight around my wrist, locking it in place. I bit back a curse.

"Imagine if every single person felt the way you feel right now, only *worse*, because I've developed a few hormone treatments that should *really* ramp up the agony. Or maybe I'll try it on the sixteenth again and make everybody want to kill each other. That'd be fun, wouldn't it?" He sighed with contentment and stood to glance back at the squawking crowds far too occupied with protecting their sensitive hairs to pay any attention to us. Then he clucked at me. "Well, no point wasting what advantage I have monologuing. Up you go!"

He wasn't thinking, not really. He bent down and grabbed me—net and all— but his arm brushed up against my hand.

Gritting my teeth, I dug my fingernails into his wrist. "You want lady business?" I snarled. "I'll show you lady business."

I'd never tried psychic imprinting a physical sensation before, but I focused right on him and projected the hell out of every ache, pain, cramp, spasm, chill, and throb. I dialled it up as loud as I possibly could and sent it straight up his arm and into his head. He crumpled with a squeal and dropped me.

He writhed beside me, clutching his gut as sweat glittered on his brow.

"You like this, huh?" I said. "Don't you just feel fan-freaking-tastic? Don't you just want to run a marathon or something?"

Terachno whimpered, but to his credit, he kept his mouth shut.

Melody sprinted up, still swatting Pluck-U-Bots off her clothes. They'd done a number on her eyebrows, leaving just a few scraggly hairs and a lot of tender skin. There was no perky smile as she pulled out her trusty pocketknife and started sawing through the net's cords. After she helped me to my feet, she gave Terachno a ruthless kick in the side.

"Are you okay?" I asked, and she nodded, taking a deep breath as she smoothed back her ponytail.

"I'll live. Little buggers are actually pretty easy to squash, if you hit them hard enough. What about you?"

I was primed to growl something negative, complain about aches and pains and headache, but even before I said anything, I realised it wasn't true. Oh, I still had a headache, and my back still ached, and I still felt like I'd been stomped on by Terachno's Madonna a few times, but somehow none of it was as bad as it had been this morning. Terachno twitched on the ground, alternating between bracing his back and keeping steady pressure on his stomach.

Melody helped me down the steps as Nancy Franklin clicked up to us. She had mostly escaped the bots, or at least it seemed that way until I noticed her oddly stilted gate and the hand that casually flitted to put pressure against the left side of her groin. After that, I couldn't help feeling a little sorry for her. "Well done, Kinetic," she said through her teeth. "I think we can take it from here."

"What'd you do to him?" Melody asked as we walked back towards the bus stop.

"Just a little psychic imprinting. I gave him quite a load, but it'll probably wear off in a few days. Still, it should make him think twice before engaging me at this time next month."

Melody's bald brow lifted, and the smile flickered back. "Hey! You're not leaking!"

"I don't feel half so bad as I did before, either," I said.

"You think..."

I shrugged and glanced back as a group of cops with strange bald spots descended on Terachno, none too kindly twisting him over and cuffing him as he cried out. I swore I saw tears on his cheeks.

"Maybe I should do this every month," I said, almost laughing. "My dad and neighbours would thank me. And with all the pain and annoyance Terachno causes, wouldn't saddling him with this once a month kind of make things more even?"

"He's like a city-wide period, isn't he? Every month, he strikes, and everybody feels like crap until he goes away."

"Would take him off the circuit for a week."

"I know *I'd* thank you."

I smirked as we crossed onto the sidewalk. The barista bounded up, a brand new latte in his hands. His beard was a little thinner on the right cheek, and a crushed bot still dangled from the man bun, but otherwise, he was as cute as ever. "That was... awesome," he said. "I'm, I'm sorry about before. You know. Wasn't my idea."

I could have forgiven him anything at all in that moment. All I wanted was for him to scoop me up, carry me home, and let me snuggle against those tee-shirt swaddled pecs for the next few days while he hand-fed me squares of dark chocolate. But instead of breaking every rule and tearing off my mask right then and there, I simply took a drag of the salted caramel mocha latte and grinned at him, the tip of my tongue pinched between my teeth. "Maybe we'll bump into each other again sometime, hmm?"

His eyes lit up as he stepped back to let us pass, a cute little wave hovering at his side. I fluttered my fingers back at him. Melody rolled her eyes and guided me to the bus stop.

"You really should think about getting on the pill," Melody said, adding quickly, "not because of *that*. I'm just saying it helped my sister with her period a ton, and she had the worst cramps, vomiting, you name it. At least then you wouldn't *have* to dump on Terachno, unless you wanted to."

"Thanks, I'll talk to my PCP, you know, between all that saving the world shit."

Melody scoffed, and the cops passed us, hauling Terachno between them.

Stripped of his arachno-pack, he looked like a scrawny guy too old to be wearing the angsty trench coat.

"This is torture! It's not right! It's not fair!" he wailed as they shoved him into the back of a waiting cruiser.

I slurped my latte and smirked as the thirty-two bus rumbled to a stop in front of me. "Welcome to my world," I said, and headed home.

PLUMBUM TALONTUM

Derek Kagemann

Featured in Issue #78

The TEMPEST HAD FINISHED toying with Yegby Stocker. It spat him out into the lobby of H.R. & Stalwart, and he fell into step like something wrung out and left dangling over a mop bucket. The revolving doors carried on spinning behind him in a lazy pinwheel.

Yegby carried with him the city's mud leaf fetor of garbage, exhaust, and overcooked hot dogs. Fat droplets of rain piggybacked in on his black slicker. He was glad for the company, as unwelcome as he felt. His rubberised work boots squeaked like mice smeared across the floor.

There was a held call smouldering at the front desk and a receptionist posted there to lord over it. The man sat pensively, his hand resting on the telephone receiver. His attention remained fixed on the hot, red light, which flashed against a backdrop of vintage Bakelite and cherry veneer. He looked up just long enough to spare Yegby a scowl.

"You're the plumber now?" the receptionist asked. His mouth was a flit of salmon and stained ivory beneath the cinnamon stubble of a nascent moustache. He wore his gold and blue uniform with the conceit of a decorated admiral from some isolated banana republic, myopically confident of each petty victory.

"Finnegan Stocker...and Sons." Yegby patted himself down for a business card. He threw a handful of crumpled receipts onto the desk... a pen... his keys... a tube of lip balm with a black band of lint and filth in the gap beneath the skewed cap. Having failed to locate his credentials, Yegby waggled his dented toolbox over the desk.

"Actually, 'sons' is a bit of a misnomer," Yegby confessed. "Finnegan is my uncle, and I'm his *only* employee. I started yesterday."

The receptionist was not buying any of it. *Had not this Yegby person come in just last week working as a deliveryman, and then the week before peddling office supplies?*

Men like him checked the boxes that upstanding people left blank. Paperwork was the finely milled palisade that civilisation erected against those barbarians.

The building's sign-in sheet stayed put, just out of the dishevelled interloper's reach.

"I mean...I've worked for him before, a couple—a few times, actually. I just finished my apprenticeship. I tried my hand at other things..." A *lot* of other things, but there was always Uncle Finnegan to fall back on.

They had an arrangement worked out. Yegby did good work for six months. Honestly, he did! After that, he got bored and screwed things up. Finnegan hired his nephew for the first half of each year and then fired him, so that the kid could screw up in another city on some other schmuck's dime.

There just weren't a lot of six-month jobs these days.

"Sign in." The receptionist sighed and nudged the clipboard forward. With his other hand, he slid the cup of complimentary pens out of sight behind an understated desk sign, which read 'No Solicitors' in brass lettering on oak veneer.

Yegby retrieved his own pen, which he had inadvertently stolen the last time that someone had given him paperwork to sign. A short length of bead chain dangled from one end.

Crumpled up and discarded, with the pen strokes properly contorted, Yegby's signature was potentially legible. His unintelligible scrawl had evolved from the primordial ink but had yet to find its legs on dry paper. Water dripped from his cuff, and the receptionist's sneer darkened into an overt scowl.

"Third floor."

The hold light continued to blink. It looked angry.

"You going to answer that?"

"Salesman," the receptionist said flatly, meaning no.

Yegby squeaked toward the stairwell, leaving the man and his light to burn together.

♦

The bathroom was old enough that plumbing had been an afterthought. Yegby's first impression was that the windows had been sealed shut in some past century to break senior partners from the inborn habit of dumping chamber pots into the street.

It also had a reputation, which was why Yegby had been given the job. Uncle Finnegan had arthritic knees and a bad back, which were aggravated by cramped spaces, filthy toilets and manual-intensive labour. There were two stalls and half as many urinals servicing the entire seven-story building, so Yegby had expected the worst.

He opened the unmarked door.

The room's sole imperfection was a spattering of graffiti, which had been edited for spelling and grammar. A clumsy hand had penned, "I LuV CyNbi" in blue ink within the white grout margins of the taupe-tiled wall. A second author had made corrections in red ink.

It was inevitable that a third contributor would have added "ME 2" beside the original message. Below that, a dozen burgeoning poets had tacked on progressively scatological confessions of undying love. This exchange of verse and permanent ink, with each entry scribbled in twenty-words-or-less, was capped with the statement: 'She really does get around, doesn't she?' The original author had returned with his blue ballpoint, which had likewise been revised in red ink.

Yegby settled into the oversized stall reserved for claustrophobic senior executives. A blue sign advertised handicap accessibility, even though the third floor itself was as accessible to the handicapped as the second-floor ceiling. He lifted the lid from the basin and gently set it aside. The water therein was still and the rubber flapper firmly seated. *No demons hiding there.*

He knelt beside the bowl and traced his fingers along the bronze pipe that fed through the floor and into the back of the toilet. All of the inscriptions were solid. The circles and hexagrams were unbroken. With his right hand, Yegby rummaged through his toolbox for a ceremonial wrench. He brought it to bear and knocked three times with his head hung over the toilet bowl.

"*Plumbum talontum! Aqua jubeo!*" Yegby intoned. "Spirit, I command you, as per Article 9-15, Section C3 of your contract, to show yourself with due haste."

"Just give me a minute to materialise, boss," the toilet gurgled. Bubbles of faecal stench popped inside of Yegby's nostrils. He jerked away and crab-walked to the far wall.

All Yegby had wanted was a nice, little chitchat through the medium of the toilet bowl. The materialisation of a septic spirit was never pleasant. There was a maintenance sign propped up outside of the restroom, but Yegby shut the stall and slid the lock closed just in case anyway. This was professional business.

The pipes glowed with aquamarine radiance as the spirit clambered through them. This was a big one. It welled for a few seconds in the toilet bowl, riding to the lip and flipping back the seat in a sudden geyser of pure, fresh water.

Septic spirits were typically...well, everything one would expect them to be. Fairy tales chronicling instances of human possession had inspired many playground ditties, but were invariably omitted from any respectable book of children's verse. This spirit was as clean as filtered tap water in a nice neighbourhood. Yegby breathed a sigh of relief...

...and inhaled a double measure of grief and anxiety in its place. In the plumbing business, clean was a problem. He had learned his very first day that there was no such thing as clean or fresh in this world, just varying degrees of acceptable slathered under a thick glaze of marketing.

"I am...fired, am I not?" the spirit asked. It slapped each syllable between a wet towel and a red rump. At least eighty gallons of abstract art glass, freeform fluid dancing to a bass beat, spanned the distance from toilet to ceiling.

"There are...*problems*," Yegby said, "which I am here to resolve."

"I know." The ad-hoc column slumped with the sufferance of butter in a microwave. It listed then haemorrhaged onto the floor. "I fail at everything."

Yegby shot to his feet and struggled to find a dry patch. Physical contact was bad. Soaking in a spirit was worse. His uncle's retired friend had recently been diagnosed with cervical dampness and leaky elbows.

"Look, it's just that you've been... *rejecting* certain articles. You're a septic spirit. You—"

"I am *not* a septic spirit," it said with the inflection of a compressed sponge.

"Excuse me?"

The spirit pulled itself into an unsteady mound of ripples and whorls. "I am not a septic spirit!" Its voice was a squeegee raked over hot vinyl upholstery. "I am not a clot buster, a urine tapper, a drain sucker, or a turd burglar! I lied on my application. I am a pure elemental."

Yegby had lied to the receptionist. Uncle Finnegan had been doing him a huge favour by letting him work without union credentials after only a three-week apprenticeship. He knew enough to give pep talks to bubble bogies and scrub sprites. He was a fast learner, even if he exorcised pipe bangers and mildew demons at half-price because it took him twice as long as any competent plumber. An elemental of pure water though…*wow*.

There were stories—there were always stories. Masters of hermetic plumbing had invoked pure elementals, sometimes to repair flood damage, other times on a bet, but they were all cautionary tales. All of them ended badly. In most cases, the hapless cousin-of-a-friend-of-a-friend had tried to sip an elemental to know what wholly unadulterated water would taste like. No living being was meant to know.

"Please don't tell!" The elemental's plea was saline squirting from a one cc syringe. *Duuuh.*

Yegby stammered something unintelligible. This was one of those career-killing moments that his uncle had trained him not to worry about. Uncle Finnegan was going to fire him two months early and never let him return. Yegby would have to work the minimum wage jobs that burned him out ahead of schedule.

"Look," the elemental continued as though Yegby were still a thinking brain with a speaking mouth. "This is my last hope. I've tried it all. I wanted to be bath water, but I'm allergic to soap. I got a job at a wishing well, but those damn kids. They throw copper coins. *Copper!* I—I have allergies. I tried to end it all in a drinking cup. I made it halfway to the guy's mouth…"

His tears were the distant sound of water dripping underground, heard only as an echo. They were the uncertain patter of droplets on a windshield without a cloud in sight. Yegby had never realised before that steam pipes, toilets, kitchen sinks… Sometimes, in the middle of the night, they wept.

Duuuh.

Yegby remembered where he kept his words and to fill the distance between them with spaces and punctuation, which he grabbed seemingly from his pockets. They were battered syllables, striated with black lint, but he strung something together.

"But… you don't need…*jobs*. You're *pure water*. The…th-uuuuh… aristocracy. You've got dilutes and sediments to order around."

"Not me." The elemental gave a hearty *bloosh*, as though it had filled a bucket without time for a splash. "My fount wants me to flow up through the cracks and pool in muddied water before I ever evaporate and go to battle against the Air Lords. I'll fall one day into salty water, he says, and what would I do then? He thinks I'll marry some briny trollop and decant brackish offspring."

"Sounds better than my dad," Yegby said with a wry smile. "He traded his firstborn son to a used car gnome—the one with the dealership at Fourth and Main—in exchange for a golden fiddle. He used it to score his second wife, the princess, and now he's Duke of Ohio. Still, I've got to work at my uncle's plumbing business because dad feels guilty about my brother selling used cars."

"That's terrible."

"Only it's not! All Chuck has to do is answer a riddle to get his freedom. 'What seven-letter word becomes longer when the third letter is removed?' You can look up the answer on the Internet! But he's happy right where he is—top salesman for ten years running, company car, engaged to this girl who the gnome kidnapped and has raised as his own. And he gets comprehensive insurance with

401k. Next year, he'll be running his own dealership. Sometimes I wish Dad had thrown in his second-born to sweeten the deal."

The elemental inverted itself into a basin-shaped water form. "I really would have been good bath water."

"Trust me, it's not as dignified as it sounds."

"Worse than this?"

"Hey, a truck stop toilet off a busy interstate—that's a dream job for a septic spirit. This here is still a pretty good gig, though. For you… we need to figure something else out."

"I'm telling you, there's nothing! I've been exorcised over a dozen times for breach of contract."

You and me both, Yegby thought. Only exorcising a pure elemental… that would be a sight. The urinal flushed mirthfully, its resident spirit enjoying the very same thought.

"*Silence,*" the elemental commanded.

The urinal stilled.

Yegby gawked. He looked at the floor. Clean. The walls and privacy panels that should have been stained with mildew and snot streaks were all clean.

He consulted the logbook. Yeah, this was the stall with the problems. But the others… no record of the piss pixies clogging the pipes or overflowing the bowl. Spirits like that worked cheap, but they were temperamental. Most places, someone had to rebuke them at least once every other week. Exemplary conduct like this was unheard of.

Yegby undid the latch on the stall door and swung it open. He peeked across the room. There wasn't a check-up sheet posted by the door, which meant that the janitors weren't having troubles with mildew demons or slime sylphs. A master exorcist couldn't have scrubbed the place cleaner.

"I…" Yegby stumbled over what he wanted to say. The idea didn't feel possible. There wasn't room for it in his mouth. "What's your name, anyway?"

The elemental made a sound like a glacier cracking. It mellowed into a gradual trickle, the cadence of spring rain diffusing into the soil. Water flowed over the sides of a spaghetti pot onto the burner of a hot stovetop. He gurgled like indigestion at midnight. The Atlantic crashed into the Pacific, and the two oceans descended together into an abyss of monsters swimming unheard.

Yegby cringed. "Do you have a nickname?"

Ploot. It was the noise of a fish opening its mouth to catch an insect, or a soap bubble popping on the tip of a child's nose. "My sister called me that when we were young."

Yegby popped his lips and flipped his tongue. It took a few tries to get the timing right, but he managed it. *Ploot.*

"My name is Yegby. How about you work for me?"

"You? What would *you* need *me* for?"

"Well, how is it that this place is so clean?"

"I *hate* filth." Ploot's voice was a fire hose spraying full blast into a teacup. "I'm allergic to it. I command the impure waters to do as I bid and crush the minor spirits who dare intrude here."

"So you're perfect for the job. It takes me an hour—sometimes three—to rebuke a troublesome drain sucker. You could put him in line with a word…"

"I would squelch him and squelch him again until he flowed into the deepest place!"

"You get the idea. I can pay you probably five times what you're earning here—cash for me, animus for you—and it's a job you'd be great at."

"You mean it?" It was a whisper silent as mist condensing.

"Sure thing. We go into business together."

"My father… He wouldn't approve. It's perfect."

"My uncle will hate me for it too, but I'll cut him in on it. We'll get rich. He'll get rich. He'll get over it. Finnegan Stocker, Water, and Sons!"

♦

The receptionist hovered over his trapped call, like a child peering at a firefly in a jar. A tiny cinder mite lit the call light, struggling to relay its message and be free. It was an older model telephone, the merciless sort that wouldn't drop calls that had been held too long.

Yegby hit the lobby with Ploot at his heels. The elemental churned forward as a cresting wave trapped at its zenith. It lapped at the floor with impatience, eager to commune with the storm outside and hear the tales of raindrop veterans returned from the war in the sky.

The receptionist glanced up, a scowl dancing at the corners of his lips. One look at Ploot and his face dissolved into an expression of unknowing awe.

"I found your problem," Yegby said. He tossed the updated logbook onto the desk. "Elemental prince in the pipes."

"Yeah?"

"I'll file a 'help wanted' ad for you. Actually, I might even know a reliable urine tapper who could fill the vacancy. This guy… I had to exorcise him."

"Yeah," the receptionist said. He reached down, clicked the hold button, and set the captive spirit free.

RESOLUTION FOR A NEW EARTH

Helena O'Connor

Featured in Issue #81

T HE SOUND OF RAGGED breathing wakes me from my daydream. I'm staring at my hands and studying the lines. I like to try and remember the old stories; the little human things we told ourselves. *This is your love line, Zo, and this is your life line.* In my teens I stared and stared, as if I could will myself a better life. I often look for the break in my line life, though I never can seem to find it.

While I've been lost in myself, a stranger has arrived to sit on the cold plastic bench beside me. Biting wind whips through the defunct bus shelter and ruffles his thick, brown hair. He shivers but makes no move to pull his grey coat tighter. I see the intertwined leaves, the emblem of the eco-warriors, poking out from under the collar. There is a stir of surprise in my stomach, quickly replaced with pity.

His brown eyes are wide with remorse. "We can't stop the countdown."

The wind wails, hurling pieces of trash at the sides of the shelter.

I look away and pull my own faded cardigan closer, tucking in my wispy, brown ponytail. The wind pushes itself down my shirt anyway. The weather is relentless these days.

A withered arm hovers into my line of sight. Numbers are starkly etched in black ink across a fragile-looking wrist. The count is into single digits now. The end is literally nigh. I wonder how long is left—a month, a week, a day? I flick my eyes back to his, curious.

"A few days, give or take," he says mournfully, in answer to the unspoken question.

Resignation settles around me like a firm cloak. We've known for a long time. But despite everything, it's still hard to believe.

He nods towards my small, shiny suitcase. "Going to be with family?"

Tears threaten and my throat tightens painfully. "They never made it out of the Valley." Memories flash across my mind: intermittent news broadcasts, panic, and desperation; the sheer, overwhelming devastation of the storms. Thousands, tens of thousands, dead. "I came here to watch the launch."

I had been leaving town, when I realised there was nowhere left to go. Nothing to do, but bear witness to the best of humanity departing. But it's slow progress getting to the site in this weather.

The man's eyes grow misty and distant. "My daughter, Sara, didn't cross the barrier in time."

I think of the massive steel walls locked in place to stop the worst of the fires. Those caught on the other side had no chance. An involuntary shudder works its way through me. Thousands died to save millions, and for what? It's all going to end anyway.

"You look like her." His dark eyes appraise me until I break eye contact, hurriedly. I never could look an eco-warrior in the face for too long. It was their job to fix the damage. To stop the climate-change cataclysm. The chip with the countdown, their animate tattoo, was supposed to keep them motivated. But they failed. The guilt must be overwhelming.

"We can't stop the countdown," he mutters, more to himself than me. I've heard the pressure drove most of them mad. This shell of a man sitting next to me hardly dispels the notion.

I take a breath. We have only days left. If now is not the time for compassion, then when? "It's not your fault, you know. The damage was already done." Cringing internally, I admit what we all know, what we've always known, deep down. "It's our own fault. Each one of us. We let the planet die." Then, I let the eco-warrior look me right in the eyes. It's the least I can do.

He stares hard, trying to glean my intentions. Finally, he pulls a ticket from his pocket and tentatively holds it out. "My daughter had an important mission. It was our one chance for redemption. Perhaps…you could take her place?"

I grasp the ticket between my freezing fingers. It is a tiny slip of salvation that weighs nothing and means everything. My heart stutters and I can barely breathe. The eco-warrior takes my silence as assent and gives me an ID card for a sunny looking girl about my age.

"Are you sure?" My voice trembles and the words are almost lost in the flailing wind.

He hands me a small, silver device. "Plug this in to one of the information consoles. Promise me."

I nod, stunned and bemused. A ticket onto the Ark. It's simply not possible for someone like me. I'm not a scientist, a visionary, a leader. I'm ordinary, a sales team manager. Great at motivational speeches, but nothing special. I never even dared to hope.

He stands and pats my head with an old, fond gesture. Then he is gone, striding into the swirling dust. Disappearing, like the remains of humankind. I never even asked his name.

I scan the ticket. They've called the Ark *Serendipity*. It seems like a good sign. I grab my suitcase and lurch into the wind.

The Ark is headed for another world, fresh and new. A world that isn't tearing itself apart. A shining beacon of international cooperation built to save the chosen few, it will house the brightest and best on their journey through space and deliver them to build a glowing civilization on another planet.

As I head for the landing site, the knot in my stomach grows. Why would an eco-warrior have an interface for the Ark computer?

♦

I go via the Bronze, the district housing the darker parts of humanity. Fighting my way through the remnants of stalls and android street walkers, I arrive at Cyber Heaven. I push through cluttered corridors until I reach a dingy room full of wires and circuit boards, reeking of burnt electronics and sweat. A grimy, bearded hacker with goggles on his head looks up and smiles.

"Zo. Thought you already got the hell out of here."

"I came back to see the launch. But something weird just happened…"

Aran is the best hacker I know. He's always been a little on edge, and the current state of the world isn't helping. But he sets to work, and soon confirms my fears. The interface from the eco-warrior is programmed to transmit a signal through the Ark's life support system to execute the crew.

"The ship'll drift in space. No one to land it. To the end of the universe. Boom." Aran makes an exploding gesture with his hands and then giggles. "No more humans." A splash of foamy drool disappears into his keyboard. Sanity is optional on a dying world. I already decided against telling him we only have days left. Why make it worse?

I sit back in my chair, sick to the stomach. I want to be on that Ark. Do I have to honour my promise to the eco-warrior? After what we've done to this planet, we don't particularly deserve to live. But I don't think I can bring myself to end humanity. I stare at my hands and the unbroken life line. A messy stack of papers catches my eye. I'm looking for a distraction from my dilemma, so I pick up the disordered pile. It's the *Eco-Warrior Manifesto*. This comprehensive guide to saving the planet was disseminated years ago, but I never found the time to read it. As far as I knew, no one did.

"Aran, have you actually read this?"

"Yeah. It's all quite simple. I don't know why we never followed their advice." He dissolves into giggles again and more drool splashes across the keyboard. If Aran can hold it together long enough to do some reprogramming, I might just have a way out.

"I think I have a plan."

◆

The Ark contains the only beings to leave the planet. Below us, the Earth is ripping, rending, twisting. On the next planet, our next home, we must do better.

Determination fills my heart as the synth sleep begins to take me. I eye the others, the last humans. I understand why the eco-warrior wanted to destroy us. He had one chance to save the universe from the human plague. He saw it as his final mission to stop us destroying another planet. I don't blame him. But I have a better idea.

The sounds of the dying earth echoes through the accelerating ship. Louder still comes the sound of voices in unison. I sent the crew a message. I put the instructions from the *Manifesto* into my own words. Aran re-programmed the eco-warrior's device, and my voice will play on a loop for as long as the ship continues towards its new home. I hope they like my sales pitch.

"I am an eco-warrior. It is my job to protect the planet."

When we wake up on our new world, every member of our crew will be an eco-warrior. I feel a swell of satisfaction as I drift to sleep. The eco-warrior and his daughter did not die in vain. This time, humanity will be better.

The ship hurtles through space and ten million souls speak their new resolution to the dark.

(TRUE)

Laura DeHaan

Featured in Issue #80

Tanya the Witch glared at the robot in eir stall across the street. "Who does e think e is," she growled.

Belasco, the merchant on her right, didn't pause from hanging up his display of beaded necklaces. "You still got a tummy-ache over robowitch there? Girl, unclench your anus. It ain't good for your energies."

Donny, Belasco's friend and daily deliverer of bubble tea, piped up. "I saw em printing slips for two people at once yesterday."

Belasco grimaced. "Two?"

"That's what I'm talking about!" Tanya said. "Ey're bad for my business. Ey make *me* look bad. I take thirty minutes to hand-paint my spells on washi and ey're printing out spells on thermal paper for two people in half the time."

"Robowitch charges more," said Donny.

"Not without reason," said Belasco. "I see you nudging me, brah. Your pun was not that original."

"Robots need to charge more because they're electrical devices," said Donny, for Tanya's benefit.

"And they break easier," said Tanya.

Both men raised their hands. "Whoa, tiger!" said Belasco. "Do not drag me into your little piss party. I'm deaf, all right?" He looked at Donny for support.

Donny snatched away Tanya's untouched drink. "You can get your own bubble tea this morning."

Tanya forced a smile. "I'm just venting. A little friendly competition is healthy, right?" She held out her hand.

Donny backed away. "Bubble tea is for positive vibes," he said. "Catch you tomorrow, Belly." He made his way down Artisan Avenue, neatly sidestepping the tourist crowds already beginning to gather.

"I was joking," Tanya said, but Belasco fussed with his stall and pretended not to hear. "Well, I was," she muttered. She smiled brightly at a group of uniform-wearing students who had drifted into her periphery. "Love charms, good grades, spiritual cleansing! You all cutting class? Don't worry, I won't tell…"

She wrote an attraction charm for the first student, sealing it in a jam jar with rose water and a splash of vodka, but even as she put the finishing touches on the second student's traffic safety charm, the other four had run giggling across the street to the robowitch's stall.

Threefold Law of Returns be damned. She would *destroy* the robowitch.

During the usual 4 o'clock lull, as the tourists started to drift away to the restaurants a few streets over, Tanya sauntered to the robowitch's stall. "Hi!" she chirped. "I must have seen you every day for the past three months and I feel so silly for not coming by sooner to say hello!"

A few buttons on the robot clicked of their own accord. A moment later, a strip of thermal paper emerged from a slot. The robot tore it from eir body and held it up in display for Tanya to read: |hello|.

It doesn't even talk? Oh god, this is going to take forever. "So you're the robowitch!" she said brightly. E looked like an ambulatory adding machine with a multi-jointed arm and not particularly witchy.

Another strip of thermal paper, ripped and displayed: |so you are the witch|. E waited for Tanya's eyes to finish passing over the words before adding it to the recycling bag beside em.

Tanya flounced her hair. "Well, that's my job description. My *name* is Tanya."

A whirr of buttons and a new note. |robowitch is my job description ¶ my name is boot|.

"Boot? Wow. I didn't know you guys had names!"

|we have exactly what you give us ¶ i was given the name boot|.

"Oh? What else were you given?"

|apparently a face that welcomes interrogation|. E waited for her expression to change before quickly printing out, |i am told i was also given an acerbic nature similar to my creator's ¶ it does not endear me to customers|.

"Really? You seem pretty busy."

|i am a novelty ¶ like the coin operated fortune telling machines ¶ everyone likes their fortunes told ¶ they do not really believe the fortunes will come true|.

"Well... *do* your spells work?"

A pause. Deliberate:

|y e s|.

"Okay. Well. Good talking to you," said Tanya, as Boot continued to hold the paper up to her. "I should be getting back to my booth. I'll see you... directly across from me." She gave a little wave. Boot brandished the slip of paper at her in response.

Belasco glanced up from his beadwork. "Who won?"

Tanya shook her head and laughed. "It wasn't a fight."

"So Boot won."

"No, it did not, and how did you know its name is Boot?"

"*E* did not, and *eir* name is Boot. You must've lost if you're screwing up eir pronouns."

"*Eeeee* is getting customers only because people think eir the next Mechanical Turk."

Belasco frowned. "The Mechanical Turk was a person."

She waved her hands. "Or something like that, whatever. E thinks people aren't taking em seriously."

"You seem pretty happy about that."

"Am I?" She smiled. "Maybe I'm just glad to know I don't have to worry about em building up repeat customers."

Belasco raised an eyebrow, but let the matter drop.

♦

Back at her bachelor apartment, while the fire alarm bleeped to the general unconcern of the tenants, Tanya took out her cheapest paper and inks and considered her spell. The Threefold Law of Returns was *of course* made-up nonsense, or at least could be interpreted as made-up nonsense, but it did the trick of making her wary of casting a spell that was outright destructive. She mulled over her options—*something to do with corrosion? Sticky keys? A paper jam?*—until an old classic came to her: *kill it with kindness.* If the robot's mouthiness got it into trouble, let more trouble come to it. She'd send more customers its way, it would get flustered and overwhelmed, and people would see it as the joke it was and spread the word themselves. Meanwhile (according to the Law, which was *probably* untrue, according to the internet), she'd get more attention, too, except she could handle it. *I've handled asshole clients, asshole co-workers, asshole cops... One trumped-up POS machine is nothing.*

When the spell was written out and rolled up, she filled a mason jar with water, added a feather and a bread tab cut into the shape of a triangle, and plunked the spell inside. She watched until the water turned murky with the ink and then went to bed.

◆

"You seem agitated," said Belasco the next morning.

Tanya gave him a tight smile. "Didn't get my caffeine this morning." Donny hadn't brought her a bubble tea, claiming he thought she'd feel like something bitter. That rankled, but not as much as the effect last night's spell was having. Or rather, wasn't having. The robowitch still had a steady stream of customers, but not noticeably more. And she wasn't attracting any more interest than usual. Did her spell fail? Maybe the fire alarm had interfered with the casting.

A cleanerbot trundled by. "Morning, Gittim," said Belasco. "How's the world treating you?"

"morning belasco | like a baby treats a diaper ha ha ha | such is the nature of my job."

Belasco handed em his empty bubble tea cup. "And we appreciate you doing it. Don't let it get you down, little bud."

"it does not get me down | every day is a new adventure in splatter patterns | where would i be without the output of human waste i ask you."

"That's a good attitude to have."

"just as was given to me." The cleanerbot looked at Tanya expectantly.

She waggled her paper cup—green tea, from the people eight stalls to the left—and shook her head. "Still working on it. Thanks." She watched the cleanerbot hasten towards a family tossing dirty napkins over their shoulders. "Robowitch also mentioned being 'given' eir nature. What's that mean?"

"Seriously? Ey're robots. Ey're programmed. You can't program something that complex without a bit of your nature coming through. Do you really think someone actually took the time to put 'like a baby treats a diaper' into the code?"

"Never thought about it. I haven't worked with robots before." She tapped her cup against her teeth. "I should get to know some."

"Gittim comes by like five times a day."

"Mmmmm," she said. Belasco rolled his eyes. Neither said what was on their minds.

◆

"Hi, Boot," Tanya said. The robot stood placidly in eir stall behind a table whose only display was a tidy poster board of prices. "Are you done for the day?"

|i am never done ¶ it is the customers who are done|.

"Their loss," Tanya said automatically. "Are you free to hang out? I'd love to talk shop with another witch."

Boot stood motionless. Then, as though something was lodged under eir keys, e stiffly typed out: |all right|.

"Great! I know a place where we can talk."

Boot quivered and sank out of sight.

Tanya blinked. "Uh." She leaned over the table.

Something tapped her on her calf. She looked down and saw Boot, roughly two feet tall, holding out a strip of paper: |okay let's go|.

"You got shorter," she said stupidly.

|my legs are not very stable when they are fully extended|.

"Right. Sure." They started to walk. After a few strides, Tanya turned around and went back to Boot, who had only progressed a few inches. "Want me to carry you?"

|that is not necessary|.

Tanya watched eir penguin-waddle for a few seconds and sighed. "Up you go." The weight made her grunt and sweat started leaking from her armpits, not only from the exertion but from the odd looks the remaining stall owners were giving her.

Boot waved an ever-increasing length of eir thermal paper at her. |really this isn't necessary ¶ i am capable of locomotion ¶ surely this is an unsatisfactory solution ¶ neither of us are benefitting from your exertions|. Eir legs, what seemed to be little more than two plain rectangles of steel, extruded from eir body and gave tiny useless kicks.

Cursing her lack of a car, the DUI charges, and the judge who gave the sentencing, Tanya hurried to a deserted alleyway and set Boot on top of a recycling bin. She watched the thermal paper continue to print out and ran her hands over the robot, eventually finding the release catch for the paper.

She popped the roll out, ripped off the fluttering length of monologue and stuffed the remaining roll into her purse. Boot stopped clicking eir keys and lay motionless. "Playing dead doesn't work," Tanya said. "Trust me." She checked the map on her phone and hoisted the robowitch once again. After a fifteen minute walk with frequent rest breaks, she came to her destination: a computer repair shop. Surely, if the Threefold Law existed, it wouldn't apply to her if she got someone else to do her dirty work, especially if they used coding instead of magic.

"Hi there," Tanya said to the person behind the counter of the cramped yet shiny shop. "Are you Juniper?"

"Sure am," they said and closed their laptop. "What can I do for you?"

"My counting robot hasn't been working properly," said Tanya. "Could you reprogram it?"

Juniper looked at Boot, then at Tanya. She batted her eyelashes and tried to smile.

"What's e been doing?" said Juniper.

"Oh, it—e keeps writing words instead of numerical symbols. I just want you to rewire em to stick to numbers."

"Uh-huh. You got some proof of ownership for your bot?"

Tanya felt a blotchy heat in her cheeks. "Oh, sure, let me just check my purse." She set Boot flat on the floor and stayed kneeling down to rummage through her bag.

"And I'll need the robot's confirmation of desire to reprogram," said Juniper. "Failing that, a statement from another bot confirming your robot's malfunction."

Shit, shit, shit. "Oh gosh, I must've left it in the office," said Tanya. "I'll come back tomorrow."

"Sure you will," said Juniper. They opened their laptop and started typing with an intensity Tanya found worrying, especially with them staring at Boot while they did it.

"Okay bye then," said Tanya and fled with the robowitch under her arm. She felt em thrumming slightly, like the heartbeat of a hummingbird, an electrical current assuring her e was still awake and aware. The thrumming felt like poison in her veins.

◆

Tanya hailed a cab to get her and Boot back to her apartment and trudged up the three flights of stairs to her room. Details that she used to unconsciously highlight—*sturdy locks! Low-energy light bulbs! Windows that really open and close!*—now became conscious reminders of how far she had fallen from her former life. "A junky pile of scrap like you wouldn't even get on the listing," she spat at Boot. "'Gorgeous Ranch-Style Raised Bungalow on Premium Lot in Prestigious Area! Circular Driveway! Hardwood Floors! No Fucking Robots Allowed!' That would be my signature. Tanya Pilcross, Real Estate Broker, No Fucking Robots Allowed. Where the fuck do you get off buying property?"

Boot's legs retracted and a steel cover shielded eir opening.

Tanya pulled out her fanciest washi, the horse-hair brushes, inks she had made herself under exacting conditions. "You know how much that job relied on having a car? Being allowed to drive? And all those tiny, ha-ha office slights! 'Let's grab a drink, we'll take your car! Oh, can you hire a limo on such short notice?' Stupid, petty—!"

She breathed in. Breathed out. "I have no idea how to program," she said. "But that's what the internet is for." Leaving Boot by the door, she flopped onto her springy futon and started searching on her phone. *How to code. Reboot code. Program crash. Uninstall...*

Four hours and a dehydration headache later, Tanya was satisfied with the program she'd created. "I'll be honest," she said, "I don't know how this is going to come back threefold to me, but it can't be as bad as what it'll do to you." She went over to where she'd left em by the door and jabbed one of eir keys rapidly. "Boot, Boot," she said. "You gonna boot, Boot?" Ey still thrummed, but not as strongly. *Junkheap can't even defend itself.* She swallowed a caffeine pill dry and inked the program onto the washi, starting over twice because of the shaking in her hands.

```
while (true) {
    if (witch.exists()) {
        witch.shutdown();
    }
}
```

♦

Three a.m., fittingly, and it was done. Tanya dragged Boot under the one working ceiling light in the apartment and angled a clamp lamp to shine directly on eir paper receptacle. She snapped it open and rolled the bespelled washi up tight. "Maybe ordinary spells are incompatible with robots," she mused aloud. "Guess it makes sense that a water jar wouldn't gel with circuitry." She leaned in. "Or maybe I just needed to write the spell in hex code." She cackled, jittery from the caffeine and adrenaline, and inserted the washi into Boot. She clicked the receptacle closed.

Boot's feeble thrumming spiked, then became dead air.

She tapped on eir keys. Was it working? How was she supposed to know if the spell worked or not? Oh god, did the robot just run out of juice? Did Boot need to be plugged in every night to recharge?

Suddenly, the combined warm and cool light from the ceiling and clamp lamp seemed to oversaturate the robowitch, highlighting eir silent keys and chunky shape against the work desk, fading the surface into a dirty smear. The junky little robot seemed to be merely that: a static tool, no more worthy or deserving of hate than a doorknob or a tire iron.

Tanya rushed to the kitchen sink to retch and shiver. She didn't dare take em to Juniper. *I can't go back to jail.* The past twelve hours, five months, eight months, four years, twenty-six years; however far in the past she went it all spiralled back to the hunk of machined metal on her desk…

…next to the window that really opened and closed.

She staggered over, wrenched it open and shoved Boot onto the street.

E clanged loudly, crunchingly. She threw up what remained and passed out.

♦

It was past noon by the time Tanya woke up, past one by the time she showered, and past two by the time she ventured outside to her stall on Artisan Avenue. There was a small crater in the sidewalk under her window, but no other sign of the violence she'd committed last night.

At her stall, she folded up her table. Across the street, Boot's stall was unoccupied.

Belasco ignored her the entire, pitifully small time it took to collapse the legs and snap the table in half. She lingered near him, but he didn't even bother pretending to fiddle with his beads or his phone.

Eventually, she said, "Aren't you going to say goodbye?"

He folded his hands. His tone was even. "You've been working next to me for five months and you have never, not once, asked me how I was doing."

"I'm sorry," she said feebly. "How are you doing?"

"I have ocular cancer," he said. "Goodbye."

♦

Two and a half years later, Tanya finished her early shift at Dinky's Diner and wandered over to Artisan Avenue. Although the diner was only a few streets away from her former witching grounds, it was the first time she'd had the courage to go back.

To her surprise and relief, Belasco was still at his stall selling beaded necklaces, although he'd branched out to rings as well. "Hi," she said timidly once he finished ringing up a customer.

"Hi," he said, and did a double take. "Hi," he repeated, cautiously.

She gestured awkwardly. "How's your eye?"

He tapped it right on the iris. "Still glass."

"Oh my god! How long—?"

He shrugged. "Ten years, give or take—oh," he said.

"Yeah, *oh*! 'I have ocular cancer, bye,' *oh*!"

"It's not like you came to check up on me after."

She hung her head. "Yeah. I really fucked up, in a lot of ways. I'm sorry." She nodded to the rings. "Those are new?"

"Yeah, I got into silversmithing last year. It doesn't strain my eye as much." Two couples shouldered forward to ask about techniques and sourcing. Tanya stepped back and eyed the stall that used to be hers. An old man selling tiny watercolours perched on a stool and read a book, occasionally pausing to dab a pinhead-sized drop of paint on a nearby canvas.

"What are you up to? Still witching?" Belasco asked.

She blinked back to attention. "No. I haven't ever since I quit here. I got a job at Dinky's on Millerrun. Started off washing dishes, moved up to salads. Now I'm on egg duty. I bartend a few nights a week, too."

"Sounds like you're keeping busy. You know, if you really want to spend the day kissing ass and making up..." He pointed behind her. "You better get in line."

She turned. She'd tried not to look at it on her way to Belasco, but it was hard to ignore the crowd that gathered around...

"*Boot?*"

"I do not need to know what happened," said Belasco. "I do not want to know. But it doesn't take an adding machine-cum-robowitch to put some amount of two and two together."

"Well, damn. Take care, Belasco." He waved her away and she added herself to the back of the crowd.

It wasn't a magic show. Nobody oohed or ahhed, and while there was laughter, it was between friends telling jokes and not at the expense of the chunky, clunky Boot who dispensed foot after foot of thermal paper for serious-faced customers who nodded gravely at the print-outs.

Tanya was sweating long before she reached the head of the line. "Do you remember me?" she said.

With no face, no eyes, nothing that would light up in recognition, Boot looked her over. |yes|, e printed.

"I am so sorry. I don't want to take up a lot of your time, but please, tell me. What happened?"

|you were a very selfish broken human who inadvertently fixed herself|.

She wiped tears from her eyes. "Not to me, you dingus. What happened to you?"

|i was pinging out a distress signal the entire night ¶ after you dropped me out the window other robots came to help me ¶ ey hammered out the dents and tidied up the runic failsafes engraved in my chassis ¶ ey brought me to juniper who fixed my coding ¶ they were very amused by your efforts at combining witchcraft with programming|.

Tanya pointed to a specific line. "Runic failsafes?"

|against witchcraft ¶ i anticipated backlash from the witch community so i installed countermagic protocols and engraved protective charms to boot|. E tore out this message for her to read, and added, |ha ha ha|.

She stared at em in wonder. "You weren't always a witch?"

|it was not in my original programming no|.

Her head began to throb. "But you reprogrammed yourself to be a witch."

|yes|.

"And when I wrote you that new program…"

|you were essentially running an uninstall which still being a spell came back to bite you threefold on your hinder|.

"Shit," she said, with feeling. "Maybe I should've skipped witchcraft and stuck to C++."

|maybe you should keep the line moving if you are not here to purchase a spell|.

She put her hand to her mouth, laughing while crying, and blew Boot a kiss. She nudged her way through the crowd and stood on its outskirts while her thoughts looped on themselves like a faulty piece of code.

She had changed since that night. How much was real? How much was a failed spell? Was she in her heart a better person, or could a stray piece of magic ruin what good had sprung up from her falsehood?

A stranger tapped her on her shoulder. "The robowitch said to give you this," she said. She held out a strip of thermal paper.

|any sufficiently advanced magic is indistinguishable from technology|.

"Fucking robots," Tanya whispered.

THE FLAME

GB Burgess

Featured in Issue #79

ON THE OUTSKIRTS OF town, the river burnt with a thousand candle flames.

Fia walked with her parents through the cobbled street, raising her skirt and moving slowly to compensate for the unusual darkness that smothered the town. As was tradition on Need Night, lanterns in the surrounding cottages, shops and street lamps had been extinguished, leaving the nearby river as the only light source, a bright beacon for the gods.

"Will the gods answer our needs this year?" Fia's question echoed around the empty street.

"The gods are watching," her father's shadowy bulk murmured.

"They see and hear every need on Need Night," her mother added, her whisper as insignificant as her thin, vague silhouette. "The gods know our town's plight."

Neither answer fitted Fia's question. The gods might watch, see, hear and know, but that didn't mean they'd aid the town. They hadn't helped as summer crops failed and winter fever stole lives.

"Many people wished for health at last year's Need Night," Fia said. "Now they are in the ground. If the gods ignored our needs then, why would this year be different?"

Silence drew out, heavier than the dark night.

"Our needs are greater this year," Fia's mother finally said.

"Travellers have come from far away to place Need Candles on our river," her father added. "The water burns brighter than ever before. The gods won't miss our needs this time."

Fia lifted her eyes to the river on the other side of town. It really did burn brightly. The travellers' candles surely outnumbered the locals' offerings twice over. Was that a good thing? The visitors attended not out of concern for the ill, but because they liked the town's crops. The visitors missed their vegetable soups and salads. What if the gods despised such shallow needs and ignored the town for another year?

Fia gripped coins, money she'd saved towards a shop she dreamt of opening with Bren, a boy she'd schooled with. Instead of studying sums, together they'd discreetly practised calligraphy for hours on end. Coupled with the skills Bren learnt while working in his family's papermaking business, they had everything they needed to create high class invitations, cards, and books.

Secretly, Fia hoped for Bren to be more than a business partner, but thanks to the town's ill luck, they hadn't seen each other since completing their schooling. There was no time for love or even shops when plants and people died in bulk. Instead of a business, Fia would buy a high-quality Need Candle.

"What colour candle should I place on the river?" she asked. "Green for crops? Blue for health?"

"That is your choice," her mother said. "Only you know your heart's greatest need."

"I'm placing gold for happiness," her father said. "To be happy, I need crops and health, so it's a sneaky way of asking for three needs."

Fia's mother quietly laughed. "Hopefully, the gods will admire your cheek."

As they walked on, Fia continued debating her Need. Health was vital, but so was a good harvest. Maybe her father was right to choose gold. Happiness covered every angle. Or was it too vague, too hard for the gods to interpret? She was still seeking a solution when the darkness softened, the river of candles eating the night.

Fia and her parents left the building-lined streets, stepping onto a cleared stretch of land by the riverside. The whole town crammed together there, facing the glowing river, and an eerie silence lurked all around. Normally, Need Night brought cheer and light, fluttery chatter born from renewed hope. All Fia sensed was weariness.

Following her parents, she moved through the crowd, tiptoeing to see the water. It was beautiful, lit with a mass of floating candles that drifted slowly downstream. It was also a little sad. Normally, the small flames sat atop an array of coloured candles. Blue and green for health and harvest, purple and white for wisdom and childbirth, gold for happiness and red for love. But the only colours visible on the river were blue and green. Not a single soul had room for knowledge, children, happiness or love. It weighed Fia down, making her drag her feet.

"Come, Fia." Her mother coaxed her through the gathering, zig-zagging towards the closest candlemaker stall.

Adeen, who'd schooled with Fia, sat behind a counter. Spread before her were coloured candles of every shape and size. As Fia and her parents approached, Adeen smiled. "It's good to see you all in fine health."

"You too, Adeen." Fia recalled the news that had reached their farm days earlier. "How is your betrothed? We heard the fever found him."

Adeen's smile faltered, but quickly strengthened again as she squared her shoulders. "Fulki is strong. He'll be fine." She gestured to the candles. "What Need will aid you this night?"

Fia's parents purchased gold candles. They were modest in size and quality, and wouldn't burn long, but they'd stand out amongst the mass of green and blue. The gods would surely see them.

"Go on without me," Fia suggested. "I'll chat with Adeen before I join you."

When her parents moved away, Fia gripped Adeen's hands. "I'm terribly sorry to hear about Fulki. You were inseparable at school."

"That will remain unchanged," Adeen said calmly. "There is no need to grieve for Fulki because he's going to survive." She leant forward and whispered. "I placed more than one health candle on the river."

Fia gasped. Only one candle was allowed. To cheat the gods could bring misfortune.

"I broke no rules," Adeen hurried on. "I placed my candle, one for Fulki and others for friends too ill to travel to the river."

"They asked you to?"

Adeen jutted her chin. "If they were able, they would."

Fia looked in every direction, fearing reprimand from the gods. A sudden rain that would extinguish the candles or a savage lightning strike. "We must keep the gods happy, Adeen."

Adeen shrugged. "They aren't the only strength we have to draw on. If the gods fail to help Fulki, our shared love will be medicine enough."

Adeen's gaze burnt as brightly as the river, tempting Fia to believe her. Could love be that strong? She'd seen it strengthen her parents as their crops withered, and the neighbours remained hopeful even after burying their child. Love truly was a powerful tonic.

"I considered placing another candle," Adeen said.

"For who?" Which poor soul had joined the list of sick and dying?

"Bren Riddell."

Typically, mention of Bren filled Fia with warmth, and a blush would burn her cheeks. This time his name shot ice shards through her insides.

"Bren is sick?"

"Not at all," Adeen said quickly, "but his parents took ill last night. I doubt he'll make it to the river, too busy tending their fevers."

"I must help him," Fia blurted.

Adeen's mouth twitched with a flicker of a smile. "I thought you might feel that way. You were terribly shy at school, but I wondered if you held a flame for Bren."

Fia was shy when it came to boys. Thoughts of Bren often swirled through her mind, but they never made it to her tongue. She breathed deeply, determined this time to say aloud the truth. "I hold more than a flame for Bren. He sets my soul afire."

Years of classroom fantasies of opening a business together had gradually turned into gentle flirtations. Lingering looks. Smiles. The 'accidental' brush of fingers as they reached for the inkwell. They were subtle gestures compared to the kisses Adeen and Fulki flaunted whenever the teacher wasn't looking, but they'd meant much to Fia.

"Despite plans to work together, I've seen little of Bren in the last grim year." Fia lowered her eyes to avoid Adeen's gaze. "A boy like Bren has likely forgotten the farmgirl who corrected the shape of his letters."

"I see Bren at the market," Adeen said. "He sells paper beside my honey and candle stall. I have seen no sign of another girl in Bren's life."

A smile crept onto Fia's face. Guilt quickly dissolved it. "Shame on me for feeling joy when Bren's parents lay ill."

Adeen frowned. "Is there a rule you can't feel happy and sad at the same time? I see bodies carried from houses and it saddens me, yet I still laugh each evening with Fulki." She gripped Fia's hands. "Don't waste time debating the rights and wrongs. Grab every opportunity that comes your way."

Fia giggled behind a hand. "Like you often grabbed Fulki at school?"

"Exactly," Adeen said. "Now the future is so uncertain, don't you wish you'd done the same to Bren?" She gestured to her candles. "Choose a Need, Fia. What would you most like to ask of the gods?"

Fia ran her eyes over the colourful collection. There was everything: tiny candles suitable for infants' wishes, basic balls and cylinders, novelty shaped lotuses, swans and butterflies, and large sculpted dragons that would burn for days.

"Which one?" Adeen said. "What do you need most?"

♦

Fia's heart thumped as she approached the riverbank. It felt as if every eye tracked her approach. It wasn't so far-fetched to think so. The red candle she clutched stood out.

Red for love, for her love for Bren. It wasn't the largest or most expensive candle, but it seemed the perfect choice, shaped to look like a folded, paper boat.

As a boy, Bren had sent paper boats down the river with messages written on them for Fia. She spent hours on the riverbank, aching to read the words written just for her. She never found one, the boats likely sinking or snagging on rocks and weeds, but it didn't stop her seeking them, nor Bren sending them.

She hoped the wax boat would fare better than Bren's paper ones, that her message would reach the gods.

With her hands cupped around the flickering flame, Fia weaved her way to the bank, then slipped the boat into the water. It glided away, its sleek shape cutting through the current at a faster pace than the candles surrounding it, slicing between the bobbing clutter of green and blue, a scarlet streak of desire. It was sure to capture the gods' attention.

With hope and an untameable smile, Fia straightened. But the smile soon froze on her face. All around, people looked from her to the boat and back again. Mouths fell open. Eyes bulged. Hands clutched hearts. Was Fia's need for love so shocking?

Mimicking the stubbornness and bravery she envied in Adeen, Fia tipped her chin up and stood tall. "What do we have worth fighting for if we don't have love?"

After a long stretch of silence, the crowd closed their mouths and nodded.

A stranger clasped her shoulder. "It's a beautiful Need."

"I wish I had chosen a red candle," another said.

Comments flowed over the breeze, and for the first time since arriving, a tinkling of laughter.

With a last look at her boat, Fia turned away from the river and slipped through the crowd. She walked quickly, scared her bravery would run out before she could complete her plans for the night. Setting the boat sailing had been important but also the easy part. What was to come next would be harder. She squashed her nerves down with a deep breath and marched faster.

Her parents stepped in her way.

"Don't chastise me for buying a red candle," Fia said. "And don't try and stop me. I'm going to Bren's house."

"We only want to wish you luck," her father said.

"Not that you'll need it," her mother added. "Bren will be lucky to have such a determined young lady."

They hugged her, then pressed their hands to her back, sending her on her journey in the same way she'd set her wax boat free.

◆

Halfway to Bren's, Fia broke into a run. By the time she arrived, her heart raced with a wild mix of exertion and nerves. She pounded the door before remembering Bren's sick parents.

"I'm sorry for the disturbance," she blurted before the door fully opened. "Oh." She expected to see Bren, but instead faced Bren's neighbour. "I apologise for visiting so late," Fia continued. "Would Bren be available? I know he's busy, but if I could steal him for just one moment…"

The woman's down-turned mouth silenced Fia. She knew that look. She'd seen it many times in the past year.

"The fever burnt fast," the woman said. "Bren's parents died."

Head swimming, Fia gripped the doorway. "Please let Bren know how sorry I am." Her throat closed around a hot ball of grief as she stepped away from the door.

"You're Fia, yes?" the neighbour asked. "You and Bren were once close. I'm sure he'd gain comfort from your visit." She caught Fia's arm and drew her inside.

They passed through a room lit by a small fire. Fia caught glimpses of the lives lived in the structure. An incomplete cross-stitch. A book parted in the middle with a feather. Projects that would remain forever unfinished. Fia looked away, ashamed she'd wasted her Need on love. A blue boat might have reached the gods in time to save the Riddells.

"Bren is in the yard." The neighbour led Fia to a back exit, coaxing her into a garden.

The garden should have been cosy with its tall hedges creating privacy and a choir of frogs croaking around an ivy-smothered pond, but the sight of Bren made Fia tremble.

He stood by the pond with his head bowed and hands locked over his chest. Most of his face was masked by caramel curls he'd always worn at a daring length. Fia had often dreamt of running her hands through his hair but hadn't found the courage. And now it would never happen. Once he knew how she'd wasted her Need Candle on love instead of helping his parents, he'd hate her.

She froze mid-step. She didn't want to tell him what she'd done and dreaded his look of disgust. Besides, he probably wanted to be alone with his grief. Convincing herself it was the right thing to do, she stepped away. A twig crunched beneath her foot.

Bren raised his head. "Fia?" His eyes were glazed, coated with shock. Fia's neighbours had looked the same way when their child died. "Are you really here?"

Fia lowered her eyes, shamed. He was right to ask if she truly had the audacity to visit at such a dark time.

"I won't stay," she said. "I just want to offer my condolences. Your parents were always kind to me."

Yet she'd refused them a health candle.

"Bren, I'm sorry," she blurted. "I had the coins to buy a grand blue candle, but I sent a red paper boat replica down the river instead. I'm selfish and appalling."

"A red boat?" Bren's voice was unusually husky, likely hoarse from sobbing. "Who was it for?"

Fia wanted to run away but she'd already denied Bren so much with her poor choices. The least she could do was answer truthfully. She faced him and met his eyes in the slowly building moonlight.

"It was for you. I…" She breathed deeply. "I love you."

Bren frowned. "You didn't need to send a red candle down a river. You could have just told me."

If only it was that simple. Or maybe it was, and she'd been too foolish to realise it.

"I wasted my Need begging the gods for love," Fia said, "when I should have bought the biggest blue candle and saved your parents."

Tears fell but she swiped them away. She had no right to cry. She deserved to have the pain of grief bottled inside her forever. And likely she would. Bren's hate would cause her endless misery.

"A million blue candles wouldn't have saved my parents, Fia," Bren said. "They died this morning, long before the first candle was lit. Their deaths aren't your burden."

Relief washed through Fia. It didn't dissolve the grief she felt for Bren's parents, but at least Bren didn't hate her.

Bren smiled, the expression somehow warm despite his grief-addled eyes. "The boat candle was a beautiful gesture."

Fia shook her head. "No, it was foolish. All the candles are foolish. They do nothing to help us. The gods, if they exist, ignore our needs."

Bren's smile strengthened. "Oh, Fia, I have always appreciated your thoughts and feelings, but this time you're very wrong. The gods are listening, and they do answer our needs."

Fia tilted her head. How could he have such faith after losing his parents to a fever the gods allowed?

"My parents knew they wouldn't see this Need Night," Bren said. "Their last request was I purchase candles on their behalf and set them afloat. I couldn't face the crowded river, but I hoped if I lit them on this pond, the gods would still see. It appears they have."

He shifted a tangle of ivy aside, revealing three candles burning on the pond. Red candles.

"My parents wanted me to be happy," Bren said. "They knew what I needed."

"What do you need?" Fia croaked, fear and hope twisting, choking her.

"I need you, Fia."

Fia hesitated. "As a business partner? For my Calligraphy skills?"

Bren laughed. "For far more than that." He held out his hand.

Fia sent a silent thanks to the gods, slipped her hand into Bren's and faced the pond. The flames flickered, dancing. "The gods listened for once."

"Yes," Bren said. "It might be the first Need the gods have filled in a long while, but it won't be the last. The gods have finally found us. They'll bring crops, health and plenty of love." Bren squeezed Fia's hand. "We have a bright future ahead of us."

Fia rested her head on Bren's shoulder and together, they stared into the flickering flames.

ALL THE STARS IN HER EYES

Deborah Sheldon

Featured in Issue #80

JANET AND HER DAUGHTER sing nursery rhymes at bath-time. The last nursery rhyme must always be *Twinkle, Twinkle, Little Star* because that is Aurora's favourite. Aurora is three years old. As she sings, she waggles her fingers to imitate her mother, unknowingly mimicking the shimmer of distant suns. Janet feels both a rush of love and the anxious sensation that time is fleeting. She grabs her phone from the pocket of her dress and takes a photograph. Aurora, used to posing, widens her eyes and purses her lips.

The flash goes off.

Janet inspects the photograph. It is a good one. She will email it to her sister, Megan, who lives in Perth on the other side of Australia. Megan has not yet met Aurora. Neither sister can afford the airfare. They are both young, in their twenties. Megan is a waitress. Since becoming a single mother, Janet—the promising and talented graphic designer—has worked from home, freelance, designing book covers and selling them via her website because she can't afford childcare. She makes enough to pay the mortgage, put food on the table, clothes on their backs, petrol in the car. But not much else. She tries not to think about the future.

Janet is about to email the photograph when she notices something odd about it. She zooms in on Aurora's face. The child has brilliant blue eyes, like those of her father, which is unsettling because Janet's eyes are brown, and Janet remembers from high-school biology that blue is a recessive trait, and brown is dominant. She reminds herself, frequently, that she must be mistaken, and while the truth is only a Google-search away, she will not investigate. Janet studies the picture. Aurora's pupils are sparkling as if filled with glitter. This must be a photographic glitch, similar to red-eye. Janet knows that red-eye is the flash reflecting on the retina. She puts the phone back in her pocket.

"Look at Mummy," she says.

"I am," Aurora says, and splashes the bath water. The rubber ducks toss in the surf.

"No," Janet says, and holds her daughter's chin. "Make your eyes big and look at me."

Aurora does so, giggling, as if they are playing. Janet's stomach tightens and falls. There are tiny specks in Aurora's pupils. Hundreds of them. Thousands of them.

Each pupil resembles a snow globe, but the specks are suspended, unmoving. Fixed. Janet tries to remember if Aurora's eyes seemed unusual in any way prior to bath-time. She thinks back to dinner, just an hour ago. Wouldn't she have noticed? It doesn't seem possible that something so catastrophic could have happened to her daughter's eyes in so brief a time. Because this must be catastrophic. Aurora is going blind. Her retinas have come loose and are floating, disintegrating, shedding their light-sensitive cells.

"Let's go," Janet says, and hoists Aurora from the bath.

"Where?"

"Into town."

"No, Mummy, it's time for sleeps," Aurora says, with reproach. Janet recognises the tone as the same she uses herself when the occasion calls for discipline. Now she must keep the panic out of her voice or else frighten her daughter.

"It's a game," she says. "A bit of fun. Come on, let's get you dressed."

Janet's poky two-bedroom cottage is twenty minutes from the town centre, including long stretches of highway with a posted speed limit of 110 kilometres an hour. At first, the roads are gravel and there are no street lights. It is a cloudless night in Melbourne's spring. The air smells of wild daisies; pungent and sickly sour. From her car seat in the back of the sedan, Aurora chats about the dark. Janet has never driven her daughter anywhere at night before. The unmade roads, lined with ditches and eucalyptus trees, are too treacherous. Aurora seems happy. Whatever is happening to her eyes must not hurt. Janet has to keep lifting her foot off the accelerator and reminding herself to breathe. The town hospital feels so far away.

She ignores the parking restrictions and cuts the engine directly out front of the casualty department. Running inside, the walls and floors beaming with harsh fluorescent lights, Aurora joggles against her chest. Janet holds the toddler against her instead of propped, as usual, on one hip. The urge to scream is powerful. Janet gulps it down.

Two nurses rush over. Their urgency spikes Janet's fear. Yet they must be reacting to Janet's demeanour, her body language. She must look pale. All the blood has left her skin and is pulsing red-hot in the core of her body.

"Help us," she says, as one of the nurses takes Aurora. "Her eyes. My daughter's eyes."

Aurora is crying. Howling. Panic is contagious.

♦

They get home sometime after 3 a.m. Both sleep until mid-morning, deaf to the raucous squawks of wattlebirds, the mewling demands of baby magpies trailing after their mothers in the long grass. Aurora, cranky, eats toast while Janet talks on the phone to Megan.

"What's it called again?" Megan says. "Hang on, I'm writing it down."

"Asteroid hyalosis. No one knows why it happens." Janet consults the print-out sheet they gave her at the hospital on discharge. The consultants dragged the town's resident ophthalmologist out of bed to confirm Aurora's diagnosis. "It's caused by globules of calcium and fats in the vitreous humour."

"And what's the vitreous humour again?"

Janet scanned the sheet. "The clear liquid that fills the eyeball."

"So, you're sure it's not serious?"

"Asteroid hyalosis doesn't affect eyesight, so they reckon. If it does, they can do an operation called a vitrectomy. They use a needle to drain off the vitreous humour—"

"Jesus, what the hell—?"

"—and replace it with salty water. Over time, the body replaces the water with fresh vitreous humour. Apparently, there's no damage from the condition or the treatment."

Megan remains silent. Janet suspects that she knows what her sister is thinking. Waiting, Janet listens to the line's hum and crackle. Her raw nerves move in concert with the random tide of noise. Through the open doorway, Aurora crumples a piece of toast in her hand and mashes it against her mouth. Aurora seems okay. After the initial fright, she drowsed through most of the examinations at the hospital, through the poking and prodding, the tests.

Asteroid hyalosis afflicts not just humans but dogs, cats, horses, and some type of animal called a chinchilla. The condition affects one in 200 people, but Janet finds this hard to believe. She has never seen it before. Except for once. And, with help, she had long convinced herself that she either imagined or dreamed it.

"Are you still there?" Janet says.

"Yeah, I'm still here. I'm…oh shit, I dunno, I'm just… Do you need me to come over?"

Janet slumps against the kitchen bench. "Thanks, but it's too much money."

"I could borrow some. Pull some extra shifts. I can do it. Be there tomorrow."

Janet's eyes fill with tears. "No. Just having you to talk to is enough."

"Really?"

"Really." Janet bites at a thumbnail. Hesitates. If Megan won't bring it up, then she will. She says, "Look, I asked them if this asteroid hyalosis is hereditary."

She feels rather than hears the frosty silence.

"Oh, come on," Megan says. "Are you kidding me?"

"Please—"

"If you start this again," Megan says emphatically, "I'm hanging up."

Janet hangs up instead. She puts the phone in her pocket, hands shaking.

Later, she takes Aurora into the cottage's back yard. Aurora knows not to venture beyond the patio. Besides, the girl prefers to fossick in the blue-shell sandpit. The day is warm. Janet spreads a towel on the weeds and couch grass, and lies down. Crooking an arm beneath her head, she closes her eyes.

When she opens them again, a dog has its muzzle near Aurora's face.

Janet sits up, heart seizing. She imagines toothy jaws clamping around her daughter's plump, perfect cheeks. Fear makes her freeze. The strange dog is sniffing, panting, tongue lolling, tail wagging. The dog is a black Labrador. Full-grown male. No collar. Aurora is smiling and patting the dog, crooning at it. The dog seems to like the attention.

After a few seconds, Janet finds her legs. The dog is a bomb with a mercury switch. Janet's every movement has to be careful, non-threatening, or else the dog is sure to bite. Gently, slowly, she picks up Aurora and takes her inside, sagging with relief when the screen door clicks shut. The dog stays put. Aurora remains by the screen door and babbles. The stray wags its tail, lips arranged as if smiling.

Hours later, at dinner-time, the stray has still not left. Janet considers calling the council, asking them to send a dog-catcher.

Aurora says, "Please feed him, Mummy. He's hungry."

"Good. If he's hungry, he'll go home."

"No! Give him something to eat!" Aurora's crystalline eyes film with tears. "Feed him, Mummy. Feed him!"

Aurora won't stop crying and begging. Exhausted, Janet defrosts some beef mince and puts it on a plate. She turns on the outside lamp. The patio leaps into brightness and shadows. The dog, grinning, cocks its head. It seems friendly enough, but you can't be too sure.

"Hey there, mate," Janet says, wary of teeth. "You want something to eat? Here you go."

She puts the plate onto the ground.

The dog sits up straight. The illumination from the outdoor lamp catches the gleam in the dog's eyes. Catches the multiple gleams. Janet holds her breath and forgets her fear. She approaches the dog. It watches her. Janet's legs tremble. She squats down. The animal's eyes are filled with glitter. Each pupil brims with a thousand, glittering stars.

Janet falls back, gasping. The dog hurries over to her, licks her face.

"Let's keep him!" Aurora shouts through the screen door. "He's our dog, Mummy. Ours."

The coincidence is too great. Janet realises that Aurora's father has sent this dog.

◆

She calls the dog "Comet." Comet settles into the household routine as if he has always lived there. He is a quiet, placid dog who doesn't bark. Janet likes having a dog. It makes her feel safer at night. Their neighbours are few and distant.

Aurora likes having a dog too. She and Comet are constant companions. Devoted to each other, in fact. Sometimes, Janet feels disquieted by the connection between them. Sometimes, they stare into each other's eyes, solemnly, silently, as if communicating telepathically, and it makes the sweat break out on Janet's palms.

Aurora's father had asteroid hyalosis.

The party was at a townhouse in a grotty inner-city suburb. Someone at work had invited Janet. She was twenty-two, slim and fit, and fresh from a break-up. She had worn a short skirt and thigh-high boots. "On the prowl," as she and her friends at the time had called it.

The townhouse was packed, stuffy with grass and cigarette smoke, the stink of countless perfumes and colognes. The old plaster walls vibrated from the thumping music. All the men were young, brash, cocky, loud, overly familiar with a hand on her shoulder, elbow or hip while they leaned in close and talked bullshit into her ear over the blare of music and the general cacophony of conversation, laughter, whooping. They bored her.

She met him in the laundry. Alone, he was leaning against a cabinet, drinking a beer.

The sight of him hooked her somewhere deep in the solar plexus.

Tall, tanned, lean to the point of skinny but with giant, callused hands that looked used to hard, physical labour. Boots, old denim jeans, faded t-shirt. Collar-length, curly brown hair. Square jaw with a dimple in his chin, three-day growth of beard. And big eyes. Big, sad, soulful eyes with long lashes, the irises a startling and brilliant blue. When he smiled at her, she felt it between her legs.

They talked. What about?

He told her his name. Or did he?

They soon tired of raising their voices over the hubbub, and went out the back door. The yard was a scrubby square of grass with a few dead plants and a rusting barbecue. And overhead, through a clear sky, the turning wheel of the Milky Way. They talked some more. She could never recall their conversation. Yet she hadn't been drunk. Only three wines all night. Only three.

He kissed her and she kissed him back. His embrace jolted her nervous system, his fingertips leaving a tingle of electrical traces on her skin. When he pulled up her skirt to peel down her soaked underwear, she was already close to orgasm. He entered her. As she came, she kept her eyes open and they stared into each other. She realised that his pupils held a whirl of galaxies, contained myriad suns and orbiting planets, a slew of asteroids. The earth tipped away. She felt herself travelling through the heavens at the speed of light. And when he gripped her tightly and cried out, she saw the burst of a supernova and understood that her whole life hinged on this moment: forever bisected into *before* and *after*.

She never saw him again.

Didn't know his name. Couldn't recall what happened after their lovemaking.

Megan's take on the experience: The man had roofied Janet, and the drugs in her system had caused hallucinations and amnesia. Megan had urged Janet to have an abortion, but no, no. Janet knew in the deep, superstitious dark of her mind that she carried a star baby. *You're having another breakdown*, Megan had said. But no, no. Janet was clearheaded about the pregnancy. As the stranger's baby grew inside of her, Janet welcomed being part of the Bigger Plan. She only had to wait. Keep faith, and wait.

For months after the party, Janet tried to track down the stranger. No one knew him. No one remembered him. It got so that Janet doubted her own memory of the event, but then all she had to do was run her hands over her belly. Privately, she called him Archer, the half-man and half-horse symbol for Sagittarius. One day, she would meet him again. He would return and they would be a family.

Megan grew to hate talking about Archer. *He took advantage of you*, she would say at first, back in the days when she would discuss him. *You were drunk and he took advantage.* Megan will no longer talk about him, even though he is Aurora's father. *Stop this bullshit about having a star baby*, she had said in the lead-up to the birth. *Give your daughter a regular name.* But Janet had known better.

And the arrival of the dog, just a few days ago, proved it. She has not told Megan about Comet. Megan wouldn't understand that Larger Forces are at play.

Janet is working on a series of inter-related book covers when she notices that the house is unusually quiet. On tiptoe, she moves throughout the rooms. She finds them in the lounge. Aurora and Comet are sitting opposite each other, motionless, staring, communing with their galaxy-filled eyes. Janet doesn't know what their behaviour means.

Hopefully, it means Archer is coming back.

♦

Cognisance strikes Janet in the night, jolting her from sleep, as if the truth came to her in a dream. She lies awake until dawn, watching the clock. When she pads into Aurora's bedroom, the child is already sitting up in bed, smiling. Together, holding hands, they walk to the kitchen. Visible through the glass of the back door, Comet is standing on the patio, ears cocked. So, Aurora and Comet had the same prophetic dream and were waiting for her.

Nothing surprises Janet now.

Everything is in flow.

Aurora and Comet are patient, unblinking, while she photographs their eyes on her phone. Close ups. They follow her to the study. Watch as she switches on the computer. Neither of them fusses or hassles for breakfast. While the hard-drive boots, Janet inspects the photographs. She compares the glittering pattern of Aurora's pupils to Comet's. Their pupils look the same.

Simultaneously, she feels shocked and thrilled. She wonders why she is not hyperventilating, freaking out, as any normal person might. Instead, she taps at the keyboard, clicks the mouse, searching through star maps until she finds proof. And there it is. She sits back in her chair. The confirmation takes her breath. Causes the earth beneath her to stutter momentarily, tilt a little sideways.

Their eyes show the same patch of southern hemisphere sky.

It is unmistakeable. Irrefutable. Here is the Southern Cross constellation with the blackest of black nebulae, the Coalsack, dropped within the scrim. There, the galaxies of Small and Large Magellanic Clouds, the globular cluster named 47 Tucanae, the blip of Omega Centauri. The pearly backdrop of opalescent stars. All of these spheres represented, dot for dot in their eyes, a snapshot of the firmament.

Vindication brings tears. *He's given me a star baby*, she had told Megan, yet Megan had scoffed, cajoled, bullied, and gaslighted her.

Now, Aurora and Comet watch Janet weep. Janet stops crying, wipes her face, studies further the photographs and map. Wait. Each photograph of the pupils has something extra, something that doesn't feature in the star map. A white streak. Perhaps a shooting star? Piece of space junk? A satellite? Janet searches again.

And finds the answer.

Janet's heart thuds in the back of her throat.

She scans the newspaper article, stops, forces herself to read it again, slower this time. Her blood seems to cool and still. She has found what Archer was trying to tell her years ago at the party. Found his forewarning, his promise.

The headline proclaims: Space Rock on Collission Course with Earth.

Janet leans closer to the monitor. The fast-moving asteroid called 327369 3117XI2, about the size of a skyscraper, is due to hurtle perilously close to Earth in about nine months. Unlike most asteroids, this one has a tail, probably of dust or gas. The hive-mind of the Internet has already dubbed the rock "Dino Killer." Memes abound. While NASA and most astronomers predict nothing more than an interesting night-time spectacle as the asteroid passes, flaring its tail across the sky, a few other experts, including mathematicians, claim that the giant rock just…might…hit.

End of the World cults have jumped on board.

Repent or burn, some say. Or, gather for the arrival of spaceships. For the return of Christ. Or, let's kill ourselves before Armageddon and reach the afterlife together. Each cult has a different message. It is all nonsense. The blather of ignorant people who can only guess, panic, clutch at each other and pray, gibber. Only Janet knows. The only person in seven billion, which sounds impossible, except that it is the truth.

She dials her sister's mobile to explain, trying her best to sound reasonable.

"This is insane," Megan says.

Janet holds the phone tight and bites her lip. "I can send you the photos of their eyes."

"When was the last time you saw the doctor?"

"A couple of months ago. For my Pap smear."

Megan says, "I mean the psychiatrist."

"Oh, him." Janet sits at the kitchen table while Aurora and Comet watch her, unblinking. They are both unnaturally quiet. "I haven't seen him in a while."

"You ought to call. Today. Now. Make an appointment."

"God, Megan. Really? Look, I'll send you the photos—"

"Can't you see what's going on here? It's happening again. Can't you see the signs?"

"Stop it, Megan—"

"Your Messiah bullshit again? This is crazy—"

"Come on, I want to protect you. Save you. How could you even—?"

"—raped you wasn't a goddamned alien, he was a—"

"—never even tried to believe what I—"

"—for Christ's sake, Janet, listen—"

"—can't you just—"

"No, you *listen to me!*" Megan screams. "You've got a child, and in your state of mind—"

"Oh, fuck off, take my side for—"

"You might hurt her! You might hallucinate some awful, terrible stuff—"

Janet hangs up, breathless, shaking.

♦

Despite its moniker, "Dino Killer" is not big enough to wipe out life on earth. Estimates suggest its impact would be similar to the Tunguska Event, which was when an asteroid hit Siberia in 1908. The Tunguska Event flattened 2000 square kilometres. Registered 5.0 on the Richter magnitude scale. Exploded with the power of 1000 atomic bombs. And killed just three people, since that particular area in Russia was all but uninhabited.

These facts do not comfort Janet because she understands that Dino Killer, or DK for short, will hit the city of Melbourne. She understands this at the subatomic level, within the molecular structure of her bone marrow. She understands it inside her dreams.

She has nine months to build an underground bunker. Plenty of time. And she has plenty of ground too; her cottage sits on half an acre of bushland. However, what she lacks is plenty of money. The cost turns out to be prohibitive; about the same again as her mortgage.

Which is why she is inspecting the cellar.

She has ignored it ever since moving in.

Because it is cold down here. Damp. The scent of earth is strong through the wooden panel walls. It reminds her of a grave. The floor is a poured slab of concrete, the ceiling low. Access is via a ladder through a trap door in the yard. The previous owners had used the cellar as storage space. Janet hasn't used it at all.

She kicks at the cobwebs. Roams her torchlight across the overhead beams. The cellar is small, about the size of the lounge room and kitchen combined, but it will have to do.

Besides, the shock wave from DK won't last long. She only needs to protect her family from the short-lived blast of hurricane winds that will fling uprooted forests, pulverised houses, airborne cars, and everything else in a single, titanic gust. Once the shock wave has passed, they can climb out. Rebuild the cottage. Start over.

And she will have Archer to help her.

He was a carpenter, wasn't he? Yes, she remembers that snippet from their conversation at the party. It explains his callused hands. All tradesmen have callused hands. Archer will construct a new weatherboard home for his woman, child, and dog. His message in the townhouse's laundry: *Prepare for disaster, and wait for me to come back.* She remembers. The knowledge surges to the surface from where it has lain dormant in her bone marrow.

Now to get ready. For starters, the cottage already has a rainwater tank. Good.

So, Janet's first purchase for her makeshift bunker is a food dehydrator.

The machine looks like a microwave but with six metal racks inside. To prepare food, she needs to slice the items thinly. She starts with fruit. Oranges and apples; Aurora's favourites. Who knows how long it will take Melbourne's food supply chain to resurrect itself? Janet is planning for at least three months.

"I wanna help," Aurora says.

"Not with the knife. Here, put the slices on the rack. Keep them spaced apart."

The machine is simple to operate with two buttons for temperature and time. It works as described. She stores the dehydrated fruit in labelled freezer bags. Next, she works on vegetables. She and Aurora are having fun, enjoying themselves. Janet hasn't told her about the asteroid. Comet lies near their feet, his head on his paws, twitching both eyebrows as he watches them. Periodically, Janet's phone rings but she lets it go to voicemail.

Next, she buys boxes of tinned goods from discount outlets. Packaged foods too. Giant bags of rice and dried pasta. The shelving units in the cellar are filling up with produce. She buys a camp stove and gas bottles. Doesn't bother with a refrigerator since the power stations will be out of commission. She hoards camp lanterns. Candles. Batteries, lots of batteries, and torches. Nightlights.

A compost toilet is the biggest expense, apart from paying a plumber to route a pipe from the water tank into the cellar, and put a tap on it. Drainage for a shower is impractical and expensive. They will make do with a basin. Online, she discovers portable hand-cranked washing machines and buys one. Cot beds, board games, books, puzzles. Second-hand sofa and table. Rug.

The months go by. It starts to look like a home down there. A cluttered, crazy home.

One evening, she is bathing Aurora. Time is fleeting. DK is almost upon them. Janet raises both hands, as is their custom. "Ready to sing *Twinkle, Twinkle, Little Star?*"

Aurora shakes her head.

"What's the matter?" Janet says, dropping her hands.

"Are we really gonna live in the cellar?"

Janet hesitates. "Not for a little while yet, honey. And if so, only for a few weeks."

"I don't like it down there."

"Oh, why not? Don't you like cosy places?"

Aurora pouts her lip. The blip of DK, represented in her pupils, is larger. Has been growing steadily larger, in fact, with a longer and brighter tail every day. It is now the biggest object in Aurora's pupillary night sky. Janet is afraid but excited. Melbourne will be flattened, yes, but Archer is coming back. Some days, the tug-of-war of these contrary feelings overwhelms her, stymies her, whispers for the peace and release of sitting back in a warm bath with a sharp blade, the suggestion so intense that she has to shake herself out of its lure. Comet watches her these days. Watches her closely. As if he knows. Can read her mind.

Now, she tries to smile at Aurora, and says, "The cellar is okay. Come on, what's wrong, hon? There'll be lots of fun things to do. We'll spend all our days playing together."

"It's too dark."

That's true. It is autumn. By the time DK strikes, it will be winter. Janet imagines how cold it might be for them, buried under the house, buried deep inside the earth. And what if DK sparks bushfires? What if the cottage burns above them? Kills them with smoke? With falling, fiery debris? Her resolve falters.

But then she remembers Archer. She wishes she could tell Aurora that her father is coming back. They have never discussed him. Not once. Not ever.

"Comet doesn't want to live in the dirt either," Aurora says, pouting.

◆

From dollar stores, Janet buys cutlery, plates, bowls, cups, glasses. Knives and serving spoons. More knives. First aid kits. She wants to buy an indoor gas heater but is scared of carbon monoxide poisoning despite the manufacturer's exhortations of safety stamped on the box. Yet the weather is cooling. The sun is withdrawing, rising later, setting sooner. In the night sky, Janet can see DK. It resembles a lit match-head with its blue halo.

Blankets, blankets, blankets. Janet purchases them by the armload from op shops.

She buys a small generator and stockpiles cans of petrol. She will need, at the very least, to keep her phone charged and there is no other way. Without her phone, she will be cut off.

She receives a text, an ultimatum, from Megan: I'M FLYING TO MELBOURNE.

Janet is compelled to call. It is the first conversation they have had since Megan expressed the fear that Janet might hurt Aurora.

"Are you okay?" Megan says, sounding out of breath. "Is Aurora okay?"

"We're both fine. There's no need for you to visit."

"Listen, have you heard the latest news about the asteroid?"

Janet sucks on her top lip. Finally, she says, "Yeah. I've heard."

"Oh my God. I mean…shit. Holy fuck."

Janet doesn't reply. Feels that she doesn't have to say anything. Not anymore. Not now.

"Did you hear?" Megan says. "NASA reckons it might hit after all."

"Uh-huh."

"And you knew," Megan says, her voice reedy. "Jesus, you *knew*. Months ago. Can you send the photos now? Of Aurora's eyes. And the dog's too. Do you still have the dog?"

Comet walks into the kitchen, his claws clicking on the linoleum. He stops. His expression seems to communicate something important. Janet tightens her grip on the mobile. "Don't come here, Megan. There's no room for you. I haven't allowed for an extra person."

"What? What do you mean?"

"If you come here, I won't let you in. That's all."

There is silence on the line. Eyes closed, Janet rides the waves of static and crackle, breathing, aware of the steady beat of her heart, fluxing, strumming, singing her blood.

"We're sisters," Megan says. "Remember?"

"But I'm the crazy one. Remember? Don't come here," Janet says and hangs up, shaking.

The last few days consist of ferrying belongings into the cellar. Aurora helps when she can. She has mastered the ladder; Janet no longer needs to help her. Comet is dextrous, bolting up and down whenever the trap door is open, acting more like a sure-footed cat.

"You see?" Janet says on one of the last days. "Comet likes it in here. You should too."

Aurora says nothing. She often stonewalls instead of talking. Such behaviour makes Janet uncomfortable. But what to do about it? She can't change her daughter's personality. Maybe Aurora gets this quirk from her father. Will Archer notice when he meets Aurora for the first time? Will he love the reflection of himself? Love his mirror image?

Janet keeps a variety of radios in the cellar, including a crystal set. She has thought of everything. They will be safe down here. Safe and sound. She dreams every night of Archer. He is streaking across the Milky Way without a spaceship or suit; a ghost, an alien, perhaps even a god. In a lockbox, she has cash. A few thousand. The DK asteroid will take out not just power stations but the Internet too. Electric cash registers, the tap-and-go facilities.

And she has knives.

In apocalyptic situations, the unprepared—those who assume that governments will take care of them—are caught short and turn on the preppers like Janet, stealing their food, their water. No, no. Janet can't get a gun because of restrictions and licences, but knives are freely available. Cleavers, chef's knives, a range of paring, bread, utility, and steak knives. Stashed around the cellar. Taped to the underside of drawers, hidden beneath mattresses. At any point in the cellar, she could put her hand on a hidden knife. Just in case. Because people in crisis, desperate people, can lose their humanity as well as their sanity.

Janet is a good mother. Has made sure that Aurora can't find the knives by accident.

The days count down. The world comes together, apparently, with a plan called "Defending Earth," which is devised by the signatories to something called the *Planetary Defence Conference*. Janet doesn't bother checking the Internet anymore. It doesn't matter to her what the world governments plan to do. DK burns in the night sky. It resembles a spotlight. The brightest object apart from the moon. Soon, the moon will be outshone.

Aurora and Comet are agitated. Janet often sings nursery rhymes to them including *Twinkle, Twinkle Little Star*, but her forced jollity has no effect.

"It's okay, we'll be safe in the cellar," she urges on the Final Day, carrying Aurora against her body instead of propped on her hip. She can't bear to look into her daughter's eyes. She descends the ladder and puts Aurora down. Comet follows, padding around and around the cluttered room, whimpering. The furniture, the bookcases, the shelves. Barely space to move.

"No, I don't like it here," Aurora announces, hands over her eyes.

"It won't be for long," Janet says, as she reaches up, closes and bolts the trap door.

Comet stares at her. His blighted pupils are ablaze with twin flares.

♦

DK bears down. The light show is grand, insistent. Its brightness burns through the chinks in the boards. Curiosity gets the better of her. Janet opens the trap door.

"Stay inside," she cautions.

Meekly, Aurora and Comet cower. Janet emerges.

It is after midnight. Yet the yard is alight. For a moment, Janet wonders if she has lost her mind. She steps out, shades her eyes with her hand. In the sky is a bright burn of fire, shimmering in shades of blue, yellow and orange. Janet blinks away the after-images.

Melbourne will soon be obliterated. Buildings gone. Greenery erased. Yarra River choked with debris. Janet has never been a fan of the CBD: too noisy and busy, an assault on the senses. But how many people will die? However, it is only one city after all, and the bulk of the world's population doesn't know, doesn't care, or makes jokes and creates memes.

DK is alluring, mesmeric. Janet smiles, despite herself.

She scans the sky. *Archer, where are you?* The recollection of his scintillating touch provokes tears. Not long now. Her mobile jangles. Baffled, she takes it from her pocket. She remembers how to touch a button, put the device to her ear. She hears the crackle of distance.

"We're safe," says Megan's joyful, trilling voice.

"What?"

"The asteroid. It's going to pass us by. Oh, wow. Oh, God. Can you *believe* it?"

In the glittering firmament, DK glows as red as a hot coal. Janet understands that Megan is scoffing, cajoling, bullying, gaslighting. Megan didn't believe that Archer existed, had wanted her to abort Aurora, has never taken Janet's side against the doctors and psychiatrists. Megan is evil, trying to make Janet expose herself and her daughter to Armageddon.

"You're lying," Janet says.

"I swear, it's passing right on by. Like, missing us by a million miles or something."

"Goodbye, Megan."

"Wait a minute! There's no crisis—"

Janet hangs up.

Comet is alongside. She didn't hear him on the ladder. His eyes are luminous.

There are sudden noises beyond the trees. The breaking of branches. Is that a scuffle of footfalls? *Interloper.* An unprepared neighbour wanting to steal Janet's stash. She realises she has knives on her person already, and takes hold of them. The night sky is dazzling. The bushland glows. Where is Archer? Janet scans the heavens, murmuring in prayer to him.

"Mummy?" Aurora says, for she has emerged too.

What a naughty little girl. So wilful. So defiant all the time.

"Go back inside," Janet orders, nudging her towards the ladder. "Do as I tell you." Aurora pouts her lip, stands her ground.

To pick her up, Janet must drop one of the knives. This is a difficult decision. Child or knife? Leaf litter crunches beneath the shoes of the unseen interloper. Janet must protect her family. On the other hand, it could be Archer out there. The footsteps cease. She waits. Nobody presents themselves. Nobody calls to her.

"Archer?" she cries.

DK has turned blood-red. Janet remembers the warm bath, the sharp blade.

Where is Archer? Is he coming or not? Or must she go to him instead?

Comet's eyes are communicating with her. Helping Janet to make a decision. The answer turns out to be simple once she realises that DK *is* the message from Archer. DK's purpose is to tell her exactly what Archer needs her to do. And Janet obeys, even though it's not what she anticipated. Not what she wanted. But the solution is neat, perfect, precise, and rises up from her molecules and bone marrow, from her dreams. Everything makes sense now.

"Come here, hon," she says. "Let's go and meet Daddy."

BIOS

A J Brennan —·— Author

A.J. Brennan is a Washington D.C.-based speculative fiction writer and National Novel Writing Month obsessive. Her work has appeared in *Daily Science Fiction*, *The Arcanist*, and *Translunar Travelers Lounge*. She can occasionally be found on Twitter @ajbwrites.

Rachel Brittain —·— Author

Rachel is a creative writer and Contributing Editor for Book Riot, where she loves to scream into the void about her love of all things bookish. Her fiction has been published in *Luna Station Quarterly*, *Cream City Review*, Sword and Kettle Press, and others. She lives in the Ozarks with a rambunctious rescue dog, a black and white kingsnake, and far too many plants, most of which aren't carnivorous. You can find her on social media @rachelsbrittain or at RachelBrittain.com.

GB Burgess —·— Author

GB Burgess is a writer from Tasmania, Australia. Her work has appeared in *The Overcast Science Fiction Podcast*, *The Arcanist* and *Daily Science Fiction*. When not writing, she spoils her multiplying rescue animals, neglects her devoted husband, and extreme doodles (that's drawing without talent). Find more at: gbburgesswrites.wordpress.com

Grace Chan —·— Author

Grace Chan is an Aurealis and Norma K Hemming Award-nominated speculative fiction writer. She can't seem to stop scribbling about brains, minds, space, technology, and identity. Her debut novel, *Every Version of You*, will be published in September 2022 by Affirm Press. Her short fiction can be found in *Clarkesworld*, *Lightspeed*, *Fireside*, and many other places.

Grace was born in Malaysia and lives in Melbourne, Australia. In her other life, she works as a psychiatrist. She is represented by Jacinta Di Mase Management. You can find Grace online at www.gracechanwrites.com and on Twitter @gracechanwrites.

Pete Crivellaro —·— Author

Pete Crivarello is an American writer, conlanger, and worldbuilder. He has been developing the world of Qarzeth for over a decade, filling it with countless maps, functional languages, and hundreds of thousands of words of culture, lore, and history.

Laura DeHaan —·— Author

Laura DeHaan (any pronoun) is a healthcare worker in Toronto, Canada and is currently training for certification as a crematorium operator. See the (sporadically updated, poorly maintained) website iaminyoureyebrain.com for a full listing of stories or follow on Twitter @WritInRooster (also sporadic and poorly maintained).

Paradox Delilah —·— Author

Paradox Delilah is an Australian writer and director based in Vancouver, Canada, where she pays her bills by holding a microphone above actors' heads in the film industry. She self-published her science fiction novel *The Race* in 2019, and in 2020 her short story "Where Else But Queensland" was published in *Andromeda Spaceways Magazine*. After this success she re-focused her creativity on visual storytelling, directing and co-writing the six-episode web series *Dentists*, which received official selection for nearly forty film festivals. She is now working on a horror feature script, and another science fiction novel.

Finley Harper —·— Author

Writing from Sydney, Australia, Finley Harper's short stories have been published in *Abyss and Apex*, *Andromeda Spaceways Magazine*, and other venues. Finley has also lived in New Zealand and the UK, and draws great inspiration from travel. When not writing, Finley enjoys attempting to run outdoors, watching SFF-inspired movies or dramas, playing open-world games, and keeping up with current affairs. Finley deleted Facebook and finds Twitter unnerving, despite positive past engagement, but can be found at finleyharperauthor.com. Currently, Finley is writing a series of fantasy-romance novels, with occasional short stories for fun.

Derek Kagemann —·— Author

Derek Kagemann writes about toilet magic and post-apocalyptic nursing homes when he isn't busy caring for his wife and 2.0 children. He has been published in *Neo-Opsis*, *Murky Depths*, and *Flash Fiction Magazine*. He lives in the United States and on Twitter via @DKagemann. You can also reach him at kagemann. wordpress.com.

Nikky Lee —·— Author

Nikky Lee is an award-winning author who grew up as a barefoot 90s kid in Perth, Western Australia on Whadjuk Noongar Country. She now lives in Aotearoa New Zealand with a husband, a dog and a couch potato cat. In her free time she writes speculative fiction, often burning the candle at both ends to explore fantastic worlds, mine asteroids and meet wizards. She's had over two dozen stories published in magazines, anthologies and on radio. Her debut novel, The Rarkyn's Familiar—an epic tale of a girl bonded to a monster—was released by Parliament House Press in 2022. W: www.nikkythewriter.com | F: /nikkythewriter | T: @NikkyMLee IG: @NikkyMLee

Nick Marone —·— Editor

Nick Marone is a science fiction author and editor. His first book, *Fire Over Troubled Water,* was released in 2019 as part of the eight-author, eight-book Deadset Press *Drowned Earth Series.* In 2022, he released *Space Trip,* the first of many in a new humorous science fiction series. Nick also has some short fiction published through *Aurealis, Etherea Magazine,* and *Space and Time Magazine.* He joined *Andromeda Spaceways Magazine* in 2019 and helps out as an editor, proofreader, and web manager. Visit Nick's website, nickmarone.com, to sign up to his newsletter and follow his social media accounts.

Helena O'Connor —·— Author

Helena O'Connor is an Australian academic turned writer with short fiction published in *Aurealis, Andromeda Spaceways Inflight Magazine,* and *Nature: Futures.* She lives near the coast and prefers to write with good coffee and a view of the sea. She likes exploring video game worlds and eating cake. Twitter: @HelenaFiction.

James Rowland —·— Author

James Rowland is a New Zealand-based, British-born writer. His work has also appeared in places like *Aurealis, Compelling Science Fiction,* and *Prairie Fire.* When he's not moonlighting as a writer of magical, strange or futuristic stories, he works as an intellectual property lawyer. Besides writing, he enjoys travel, photography, reading, and the most inexplicable and greatest of all the sports: cricket. You can find more of his work at his website jamesrowland.net.

Deborah Sheldon —·— Author

Deborah Sheldon is an award-winning author, anthology editor and medical writer from Melbourne, Australia. She writes short stories, novelettes, novellas and novels across the darker spectrum of horror, crime and noir. Her latest works are the action-horror novella *Man-Beast* and the dark collection *Liminal Spaces: Horror Stories.* Awards include the Australian Shadows 'Best Collected Work' for *Perfect Little Stitches and Other Stories,* and 'Best Edited Work' for *Midnight Echo 14.* Her fiction has also been shortlisted for numerous Aurealis and Australian Shadows Awards, long-listed for a Bram Stoker, and included in 'best of' anthologies. Visit Deb at deborahsheldon.wordpress.com.

Maggie Slater —·— Author

Maggie Slater's speculative fiction has appeared in *Apex Magazine*, *Daily Science Fiction*, and *The Bronzeville Bee*, among other venues. She lives in an 1800s farmhouse in New England (USA) with two half-tamed boys, her husband, her parents, and at least one benign ghost. When she has an almost quiet moment, she enjoys Haruki Murakami novels, sampling craft beer, and hoarding cheap notebooks. For more information about her and her current projects, visit her blog at maggieslater.com or find her on Instagram @maggiedot_writes or Twitter @ maggiedotwrites.